OPERATION MORYA

Written By

Mandar Bam

PAPER TOWNS
PUBLISHERS

First Published by
Paper Towns Publishers
72, Vishwanath Dham Colony,
Niwaru Road, Jhotwara,
Jaipur, 302012

Operation Morya

ISBN Print Book - 978-93-6185-727-0

Printed in India

Acknowledgments

This book would not have been possible without the support, encouragement, and guidance of many incredible people.

To my two ladies and fam – Aparna my better half is the compass of worldly wisdom, she brings a sense of clarity to my being, that is difficult to put together in words. (maybe I will write a book on it someday). Nilanjana my eleven-year-old, is a bundle of uninhibited instincts, a constant source of inspiration, she is the one, unknowingly responsible to keep my inner child alive. Together you are the driving force which fuels my imagination and energizes my creativity. Thank you for your unwavering belief in me, even when I doubted myself. Your love and support have been the foundation of everything I do.

Aiee, Baba, Aji and Baba(Aparna's Baba) thank you, for your love and encouragement.

To my friends and beta readers – Thank you for diving into this thrill-seeking espionage adventure with me and providing invaluable feedback at every bend. Your enthusiasm and inputs gave me the confidence to keep going. A special shout out to Nidhi Singh Dharma- the story was originally penned as a screenplay and it would not have been possible without Nidhi.

To my readers – This story exists because of you. Thank you for taking a chance on this book and exploring the thrilling world of espionage on the streets of Mumbai with me.

To the city of Mumbai - Your energy, chaos, and indomitable spirit gave life to this story. The idea first took shape in my mind while sitting on the rooftop of a renowned television and media company in Vile Parle East. I sipped on my coffee and watched the flights soar into the sky every few seconds from the nearby Chhatrapati Shivaji Maharaj Mumbai International Airport. In that moment, a simple question crossed my mind: *What if...this flight was carrying a VIP and it gets shot down*?

Truly, every street and every corner of Mumbai holds a tale waiting to be told, and I am honoured to share one of them.

To the intelligence community – While this is a work of fiction, your courage and dedication to safeguarding lives inspired many of the themes in this book.

To Ganpati Bappa – The Lord of auspicious beginnings, he is the sukhakarta and he is the vighnaharta, his guidance in multitude of forms helped shaped this story and he also happens to be a central figure in the book- Ganpati Bappa Morya.

Lastly, a big thank you to everyone who played a part in this journey, no matter how small. Your contributions are deeply cherished.

This book is for you all.

With gratitude,
Mandar Bam

To My Readers

When I first imagined Operation Morya, it was as a film—a medium that inspired its vivid, visual storytelling. This cinematic vision flows through the narrative, with elements of screenplay-style writing woven into the structure to bring the events to life with a sense of immediacy and tension. I hope this unique approach transports you directly into the heart of the action, as if you're watching the story unfold on screen.

Contents

Chapter 1

The Sacrifice

The night air in Mosul is thick with anticipation; several men, clad in a long-sleeved ankle -length traditional robe, continue to gather in the town square. The skyline of Mosul, now under the control of ISIS (Islamic State of Iraq and Syria), appears to be punctuated by bursts of gunfire. The bombed buildings tell a tale of this conflict zone torn between the militia and the security forces.

Among the throng of celebrants, a few of them wave the black flag of ISIS. One of their leaders, Sadiq, addresses the crowd with fervour. Sadiq's voice booms over a handheld speaker, his words carry the weight of conviction. "By the grace of Allah, our forces have pushed back the enemy and taken back Raqqa." Sadiq proclaims in Arabic. "God willing, we will soon take back the entire region that rightfully belongs to the Daesh-Islamic Caliphate."

Celebratory gunshots ring out once again, punctuating Sadiq's speech. Amidst the jubilation, however, one man moves discreetly through the crowd, his demeanour betrays the sense of urgency under his hood. As he moves, one of Sadiq's men notice him.

RAW Headquarters, Mumbai

23 September, 2023

2130 hrs

In the heart of Mumbai, within the confines of RAW headquarters, a visibly pregnant Roma Thapa, stands before a fresh batch of recruits. Projected on a screen behind her are three simple letters: WAR.

"WAR is a bitter truth of today's world," Roma declares, her voice steady despite the weight of her words. "Our country has been drinking from this bitter cup for decades. Whether we acknowledge it or not, we are constantly in a state of war."

As Roma continues her briefing, illustrations of modern guerrilla warfare flash across the screen. Gruesome scenes from the 26/11 Attacks, 2006 Train Blasts, Pulwama Attack in Srinagar 2019, flicker through the screen. "Our brave soldiers risk their lives to protect our borders, but conflict and WAR remain an unfortunate outcome of today's geo-political circumstances." She explains. "Our mission, as always, is to stop the WAR before it begins."

With a button press, the word "WAR" flips on the reverse side and becomes "RAW". "RAW is WAR spelled backwards," Roma concludes. Her gaze is deadpan as she addresses her recruits.

ISIS Occupied Territory-Mosul

In a ragged street of Mosul, the discreet-looking man, who earlier moved away from the gun shot celebrations at the town square, now enters a dimly lit room. His movements purposeful.

He shifts a trunk aside, revealing a small electronic device hidden beneath the tiles. With practiced ease, he disassembles his Glock -17 pistol and retrieves a hidden camera from its cartridge. He begins uploading a photo and a piece of code he has written on a piece of paper, just then a sound from the street catches his attention. Peering through the window, he spots three armed men approaching his hideout. Swiftly re-assembling his Glock-17 gun, he glances at the device, it is still uploading. He knows he will need more time. He hurriedly slams the door shut. The three men spot him, one of them fires at him, the bullet misses the man by just a couple of inches. The man looks at the device once again; it is still uploading. He realizes he needs a better signal strength for the message to be delivered to his subordinates in Mumbai. He rushes upstairs, with the uploading device in one hand and gun in another.

The gunmen fire a few more shots from their AK-47 assault rifles, the bullets pierce through the safety door, and the sunlight of the setting sun filters through the door. Upon kicking open the door, the attackers notice the man inside escaping through the stairs and shower him with a fresh round of bullets. He ducks, but realizes he will need to fight fire with fire, he shoots back, with his gun to hinder their advance and continues to climb upstairs. Unfortunately, the retaliatory gunshot exactly does the opposite, as the 3 attackers in pursuit now open a non-stop fire of bullets from their automatic rifles. The rhythm of the gun fire only seizes when the lifeless body of the RAW Agent tumbles down the stairs. His body is pierced with bullets , blood oozing from his body. A ping sound disturbs the silence of the aftermath. Miraculously, the uploading device had survived amidst the array of gunshots. The ping sound signalling the completion of the upload, a silent testament to the RAW operatives sacrifice.

RAW Headquarters, Mumbai

Roma continues to address the new recruits, her words a solemn reminder of the realities they face. "When a soldier falls in battle, they receive medals for their bravery." She explains. "But you will receive neither medals nor recognition, because, technically, you do not exist."

Her words elicit a chuckle from one of the new recruits, he raises his hand, seeking permission to speak. "It's challenging, but interesting, to live this life of duality." He says, "I have been married for 10 months now, but my wife still thinks I am a boring history professor. Now, who will explain to her that my version of history also involves some real time experiments with guns and grenades on a daily basis". Roma acknowledges this mundane existence of the RAW field operatives, outside of the agency, with a nod. Her gaze softens momentarily, just then a junior officer bursts into the training room, disrupting the proceedings. Roma gives him a long hard look, Milind looks swamped.

In the monitoring room of RAW headquarters, a photograph of 3 ISIS men is in focus. The central figure is Sadiq , with two more men. Roma closely looks at the photo. "This has come from Omar's ID, our field agent in ISIS strong hold. Unfortunately, we have lost all further communication with him." informs Milind. Another JPEG pops up on the dual screen monitor." **06 000 0.3 .7 000 .09 0.01.01 0.07** "Roma's brows furrow up, as her attention is drawn into these series of numbers.

"Mujhe Omar ke baare mein update chahiye," Roma states firmly, her mind already racing with possibilities. "And yes, get cracking with the code." She orders. Her eyes fall on the series of wall clocks displaying different times in different

parts of the world. She double checks her smart watch. It is 21:59 hrs IST.

As the night unfolds in both Mosul and Mumbai, the wheels of espionage and intrigue set in motion, shaping the fate of a billion plus heart beats from India. Amidst these shadows of conflict, the agents of RAW stand steadfast. They are ready to face whatever challenges lie ahead and they have to win the war before it begins- "धर्मो रक्षति रक्षित:' - "*Dharmo Rakhshathi Rakshitah*"

Chapter 2
The Shadow of Mosul

The air reverberates with the joyous chants of "*Ganpati Bappa Morya, Ganpati Bappa Morya,*" as if each exclamation breathes life into the beating heart of Mumbai city. Ganpati Bappa statues, meticulously crafted in various shapes and sizes, adorn every corner of Girgaum Chowpatty, testifying to the artistic devotion of the Ganpati sculptors. From intricately detailed idols standing tall, to smaller replicas nestled within colorful stalls, this evening on the eve of Ganesh Chaturthi, seems to paint the Mumbai shoreline with a kaleidoscope of divine forms, inviting devotees to bask in the presence of their beloved elephant-headed deity.

Mumbaikars, dressed in their traditional attire, had already begun taking the Ganesha idols home, covering the face of the idols. One could feel the festive vibe, with the sounds of Dhol-Tashe, weaving a tapestry of faith and celebration beneath the twinkling stars.

Nearby, an old police constable, Tukaram Patil, is monitoring the temporary tents being erected for the Visarjan procession, which would happen on 1 ½, 2 ½, 5th,7th and 10th day of Ganesh Chaturthi celebrations. In the distance, several boats are dancing with the choppy waves, while distant drum beats announce Bappa's arrival. Constable Patil is looking at the moon, right above the horizon, the moon seems to have a strange-looking halo around it, triggering an ominous feeling within him. Last time, when he experienced such a feeling, he ended up losing many of his colleagues. It was the night of 26/11/2008, a nightmare which left behind many scars on his soul. Suddenly, Patil's walkie talkie comes alive.

"*Kay ho Patil*! ...What's going on? Did you finally find the bomb or not?" Police Inspector Shinde asked on the walkie-talkie, interrupting Constable Patil's reverie. Patil was a bit shaken up, while Inspector Shinde continued to giggle." *Kay ho saheb*! Is the burden of the Ganesha Festival security situation not enough? Your silly pranks are only making my problems worse."

Inside the mobile police van, the police inspector and his subordinates now erupt into an uproarious laughter at Constable Patil's expense. Patil's voice crackles through the radio control. "Sir, to disrupt our city, we don't really need a bomb. You can simply spell out the word "BOMB" loudly enough in a public space. This will be enough to ignite chaos, and even a small stampede may result into death of 10-12 Mumbaikars to the bare minimum. "The policemen in the mobile van continue to laugh at Patil's exaggeration.

One of the other constables gets out of the van to buy Pan-Beedi from the roadside stall, even as Patil's voice continues to filter through the constable's walkie-talkie. As he lights a cigarette, a poster of the Prime Minister's upcoming rally at the Bandra-Kurla Complex looms beside him. The poster further juxtaposes the festive atmosphere with the underlying tensions. The surrounding street is teeming with devotees, taking the Ganesh Idols home, the rhythmic chants of "*Ganpati Bappa Morya*", "*Morya re Bappa, Morya Re*" continue to be heard, while the night shift, sanitation workers of the maximum city navigate their way, to their respective spaces, only so that the maximum city could spring back to life, clean and rejuvenated.

JNPT Dock, Mumbai

23 September, 2023

2200 hrs

Around the same time, the sprawling expanse of Mumbai's, - Jawaharlal Nehru Port, also known as JNPT and Nhava Sheva Port- One of the largest container ports in India, was bustling with the incoming traffic of ships getting docked at the harbour. A merchant navy vessel, with a naval flag of Russian origin, flutters against the strong wind. "VLADIMIR-812," the name of the vessel is clearly visible on the starboard bow, as it smoothly gets docked at its designated berth, 11-B. The Captain of the vessel, along with his Chief Engineer are hurrying around the deck, conducting last-minute checks. Under standard procedure, the Chief Engineer is arranging all the documents for verification by the Port Authority.

In the Port Authority control room, a couple of officers actively monitor the incoming and outgoing ships on the electronic console in front of them, while they can hear radio chatter in the background. "Let's finish with the formalities of this Russian ship and relish on the Paplet fry, "Officer 1 tells Officer 2. "Looks like bhabhiji was in a good mood today? Officer 2 inquires. "No re.... the cold war is still on, but it is actually better than the daily bickering of bayko (wife). "Officer 1 chuckles. "As for the dinner dabba, Zomato hai naa." Officer 1 and Officer 2 snigger, even as they focus back on the console.

Back inside the merchant navy ship, the stern voice of the captain echoes through the corridors, as he reprimands two of his men and lines them up. "You guys reek of alcohol," the captain tells off. Sailor 1, who can barely speak in his drunken stupor, protests, pointing at this colleague. "He started it. He said it was his birthday. Let's celebrate." Sailor 2 appears to be relatively sober, breaking the protocol. He then lashes out at him, "You liar!" "How many times have I told you not to drink when we're about to dock? Your juvenile actions can get all of us in trouble. Now get lost." Turning to the Chief Engineer the captain instructs, "Make sure these jokers are amongst the last of the crew to leave the ship." Sailor 1 is clearly not in his senses, but Sailor 2 just looks on. His expressions suggest that this was all orchestrated by design.

The Captain of the Russian ship follows maritime protocol as he hands over the two satellite phones onboard to the security officer at the JNPT Dock exit. Simultaneously, the Chief Engineer hands over a bunch of documents for verification. The other crew of the ship have lined up in a row. Captain glances at his crew members. Sailor 1 and Sailor 2 do not appear to be in the queue. This gets the Captain worked up. He tries to thaw the moment with the security officer. "Is it too late to enjoy a bit of Mumbai's nightlife?" The captain remarks. Duty officer muffles to his subordinate," Their feet have not even properly landed on the ground, and the buggers already have a blowjob on their mind. "There is laughter in the air. Even Officer 1 and Officer 2 who are supervising the console, can't control their laughter." Don't be so harsh on them. They have probably not seen a woman, for weeks, if not for months. "The subordinate responds.

As the laughter subsides, Officer 1 notices a blip on the electronic console. He looks closely and swiftly swings into action. "Sir, an unregistered satellite signal is visible from their vessel," he reports to the security officer. Alarmed to verify the satellite signal, the security officer quickly runs to his monitoring system and quickly dials his desk phone.

Back at the merchant navy ship, Sailor 2's satellite phone is beeping insistently from his bag. The drunk sailor is lying on the floor. He has already taken his papers and wants to ignore the call, but he knows it can only be an urgent call. He answers, "Hello..."

It is Sadiq and his 2 men from Syria. The RAW Agent- Omar continues to lie on the floor, in a pool of blood, bullet shells appear to be scattered around him. Sadiq speaks with a sense of urgency, "Mission abort... Mission abort... Information has been leaked....We have to call off "*Quadath-Ut-Allah*". The Chief has intervened, to make this call happen"

Sailor 2- Ovaise Sheikh is furious. He controls his anger, clenches his fist, and takes a deep breath. "I have waited long enough for this opportunity. There is no question of turning back now." Ovaise can hear sounds of security forces funnelling into the vessel. Without a second thought, he hangs up the phone. He changes into a t-shirt, dumps his phone into the bag. He wraps it in a huge polythene bag. The security forces , have stormed the deck already. Ovaise flies off the deck, with the backpack strapped to his back, and dives into the water.

Officer 1 notices the satellite signal moving on the electronic console and fast escaping the JNPT Dock. He alerts his seniors, "Sir, the suspect is on the move." The security officer is already coordinating with the Police and the Coast Guard over the phone, while the prominent blip sound on the electronic console emphasizes the emergency at hand.

A couple of police jeeps are on the move, manoeuvring through the crowded streets of Colaba Causeway. At the other end of the JNPT Dock, two interceptor cars are in hot pursuit. The uniforms of the security officers flash amidst the chaos of the chase. Sirens wail in the background as they navigate through bustling streets and narrow alleys. Their determined expressions betray the urgency of their mission.

Amidst this flurry of activity, the focus shifts to Ovaise, the elusive figure at the centre of the pursuit. He emerges out of the water, slips through a crowded street, and back into the alleys. He then scales a boundary wall to get on the other side of the street. A couple of police constables are patrolling the street, but he ducks in time and slides behind a trash can like a shadow. He throws a stone in the other direction to distract the police constables and scurries into another alley. A police van passes him by ,wailing its sirens, but he camouflages himself well, around a tadpatri, meant to blanket this concrete structure of the building from the incoming rain. As the police van abruptly stops, he witnesses the police personnel fanning out in the area, with a few others erecting a barricade on the road. He quickly runs across from building to building in the shadows of the night and this time jumps across a tall wooden fence. He moves with a fluidity and grace, that seems supernatural.

Then, in a chilling and unexpected moment, he almost runs into the headlights of the Coast Guard's interceptor van, but he stops in his tracks just in time and finds himself hiding in a huge drainage pipe, about 4 feet in diameter. The drain pipe appears to be a replacement piece on the side of the road for the ongoing maintenance work. Ovaise can hear the boots on the ground coming closer, he is alert, ready to strike at a moment's notice, but then the steps recede in the other direction. As Ovaise turns his gaze in the other direction, tension peaks again, as he encounters a 10-year-old urchin boy staring at him. The boy seems to have made this drain pipe his make shift residence. He has collected some leftovers from the street and is in the midst of his meal. The urchin boy is staring blankly at Ovaise. Ovaise , stares back at him, then slowly trying to win his confidence, removes some dry fruits from his bag and offers it to the kid. The child's eyes light up as he picks up a Khajoor-date. Ovaise also grabs one for himself and takes a moment to relax. The wailing sound of the passing jeep alerts Ovaise once again. This time the kid notices the siren of the police car, but he still does not seem to have made the connection between Ovaise and the siren. The kid munches on another juicy date. Gradually, the siren fades away in the distance.

After a few seconds, Ovaise rises again from his makeshift hiding place. He looks at the map he has taken out from the backpack; he is only a 100 odd meters from his destination. In the background, the urchin boy lies lifeless, strangled in what was once his home. The food lies scattered, and a date is still in his open palm. Ovaise, quickly returns inside, picks up the date from the kid's hand and pops it in his mouth. He closes the eyes of the kid, making it appear as if he is sleeping, he gives a cold look to the kid, then looks left and right to ensure, nobody has seen him, he leaps out right back on the road, and vanishes into the crowded streets of Mumbai, which are gearing up for the Ganpati Chaturthi celebrations beginning next day.

Chapter 3
The Lost Signal

The clock flickers 3:10 AM on the digital display. Its persistent blinking reverberates the tense atmosphere, through the dimly lit halls of the RAW Headquarters in Mumbai. Seated before Roma is the Coast Guard Security Officer, Constable Patil, and his senior, Inspector Shinde. They exchange tense glances. The weight of the night's events is pressing upon them.

"Madam," the Coast Guard Security Officer begins, his voice laced with concern, "We lost the signal around Cuffe Parade Traffic Signal.......it simply vanished." Roma's brow furrows, her gaze is steadfast. "Correct me if I am wrong, but isn't it your duty to report the incident to us at the outset? We are supposed to be amongst the first responders, damn it. "The Coast Guard Security Officer starts to explain, but Roma cuts him off with a firm tone,

"It has been over 15 years since 26/11, there are protocols in place, but it seems you still haven't learnt a thing ". Inspector Shinde, interrupts, "Madam, we were preparing a report only.... "His voice trails off as Roma looks at him blankly.

Roma then takes a deep breath, gets up and marks a point on the console displaying the GPS grid of Mumbai, right behind her. It shows the precise location ,where the signal disappeared.

On another screen, the CCTV footage, shows a police jeep screeching to a halt at the Cuffe Parade Traffic Signal. An interceptor car from the Coast Guard also arrives at the same spot in the next few seconds. Inspector Shinde gets out of the jeep, along with other policemen, and so do the coast guard officers. They look around while communicating back with their respective control rooms, even as some Ganpati revellers appear to be moving in the foreground at the traffic junction. Roma pauses the CCTV footage, makes another mark on a building visible in the distance. "Right there, at about 50 meters from where you lost track of the signal, is the Arabian Embassy. Her voice resonates with authority, and the imposing presence of the embassy looms into the view. Our preliminary data analysis suggests that this is the black hole where the signal disappeared. "She adds. "If you would have kept us in the loop from the word go, we could have responded in real time. "Inspector Shinde attempts to impress her, "Madam, don't worry, we will barge into the building right away and get the investigation going." Roma's retort is sharp, " *Dokyat shen bharlay kay?* Are you really such a dumb fuck...or you are pretending to be one?" Constable Patil can't help but stifle a laugh, earning a glare from his senior. Regret washes over Roma's face as she composes herself, a hand instinctively resting on her visibly pregnant frame.

"That building is a foreign embassy. It isn't your August Kranti Maidan, where you can just stroll in at any time of the day and go about your business of shutting down some random protesters, like nobody is watching." She emphasizes, "It is an international territory, governed by international laws. Neither does your uniform have any powers beyond that gate, nor do I," she exclaims, her voice carrying the weight of experience.

Just then, Milind, Roma's colleague, barges into the cabin unannounced, prompting Roma's sharp rebuke. "*Aaho Rao.... thamba zara......*Can't you knock? Or do I have to school you as well about the rules? " She scolds him. Milind apologizes quickly before revealing a breakthrough in their investigation. "Sorry madam, just wanted to tell you, we have deciphered the code........from Mosul." Roma and Milind proceed to the situation room, their conversation continuing along the way. " Milind, why are you always so over enthused? "Milind nods for the sake of it. Roma notices and counter questions *"Cricket bahut pasand hai naa tumhe? Tumhari file mein padha tha."* Milind's eyes light up, "Yes madam, if I had the proper guidance, I would have been playing for Mumbai's T 20 team today." "I understand that, but allow me to explain. , this is not a game of T 20 cricket. If you want to succeed as an officer with the secret services, then you will need the temperament of a Test Match player, because the odds are always against us and losing is simply not an option, "Roma cautions him.

Milind acknowledges her counsel, with the shake of a head, as they enter the situation room, where analysts are diligently at work even in the wee hours of the morning. Milind takes charge of the big screen, deciphering the code that had eluded them through the evening. The screen reads," 06 000 0.3 .7 000 .09 0.01.01 0.07 "

At first glance, it may seem like high school math, but they have cleverly utilized a combination of decimal and binary coding techniques to develop a distinct code. Milind explains, his voice tinged with admiration for their adversary's cunning.

The code on the screen transforms, revealing its ominous message as "QUADATH-UT-ALLAH," Roma's shock is palpable. She wastes no time in making a crucial call to the National Security Advisor- NSA. Her urgency cuts through the silence of the early morning hours. "It's 0400 hrs in the morning Roma, this better be important," the NSA -National Security Advisor grumbles.

Undeterred, Roma presses forward, outlining the gravity of the situation and summoning key figures for an emergency meeting that would shape the course of events to come.

"Hmmm, assign it a threat level 3 for now . My office will make sure that , State CM will chair the meeting , you can coordinate with the Defence Secretary and yes, make sure Munir Khan , is also a part of the meeting. " the NSA implies.

Chapter 4

Unmanned Precision

The soft hues of dawn bathe the Jodhpur airstrip. The UAV-Unmanned Aerial Vehicle positions itself on the runway, ready for its mission. In the Operation Room of the Air Force Station, Munir Khan, flanks the two pilots–one Israeli and one Indian–each one monitoring the live feed transmitted by the UAV. A team of two operates each UAV remotely: a pilot and a sensor operator.

Screen 1, at the control station, displays crisp visuals of the UAV. The soft hues of dawn glides off its shiny surface, giving it a majestic glow. Despite its slightly odd shape, the UAV has a wingspan of 66 ft, a Honeywell engine, and a fuel carrying capacity of 1769 kg, making its size akin to that of a conventional business liner plane. The blinking lights on its surface suggests, that it is ready to take off. Munir, a seasoned veteran in his special services uniform, scrutinizes the live feed with laser focus. He looks at his service watch. They are right on time at 0500 hrs, and he directs the UAV to take off. The UAV taxi's out on the runway, and it is airborne in a matter of seconds.

Screen 2, at the control station, now comes alive, streaming the live feed , relayed from the UAV. Leaving the Jodhpur Air Force Station behind, the UAV swiftly gains altitude, and the terrain below appears to be a tiny square on a vast canvas of a brown painting, made of desert sand and sparsely sprouting green vegetation. The HUD- Heads-Up Display on the screen suggests that , the UAV is now flying at a height of 20,000 ft. and it begins to stabilize. Gradually, a small settlement appears on the terrain below. Indian pilot, zooms into the settlement. The Israeli pilot locks onto the small settlement -its target. Screen 2 shows the locked target with a display message suggesting the same.

Munir has a closer look at the target, he is a little unsure. "Reset the target 50 meters South-East," Munir commands, his voice carrying the weight of assurance. The Indian pilot swiftly adjusts the coordinates, while the Israeli counterpart double-checks the protocols. Munir focuses on the screen once again. "Now" he gives the formal order. With precision, the Indian pilot engages the trigger. "Rifle Rifle, Rifle the package is away." Indian pilot responds with the well-practiced call sign. The tension in the room peaks as the missile hurtles towards the simulated target. The missile hits the target and Screen 2 reveals the explosion. After the dust settles down, the observers confirm that they have destroyed the target. The visuals also reveal that, this was a mock setup—a test of the UAV's capabilities.

Munir congratulates the pilots. The 2 pilots reciprocate a similar gesture, as they show a thumbs-up sign to Munir and each other. The Israeli pilot turns a bit to chatter with Munir Khan. His slightly angled position, revealing his name tag, Doron Raz, and hence his Israeli identity.

"Munir, sir, target precision is just one of their capabilities. It can silently hover in the air for 20 + hours at a stretch as well. It has given us tremendous success in our recent counter offensive on the Hamas. Just wait and watch how these UAVs change the rules of air combat for you guys as well. "The Israeli pilot remarks, his confidence mirroring the transformative potential of the Unmanned Combat Aerial Vehicles.

Munir has a reassuring smile on his face, when one of his sahayaks interrupts, delivering a fax and whispering urgent words. Munir's expression shifts, hinting at the storm brewing beneath the calm façade.

Transitioning from the sterile environment of the Combat Room to the gritty reality beyond, Munir's mind races with the implications of the message he has received. The tranquillity of the morning belies the turbulence that awaits him, and as he steps out onto the airstrip, a C-17 Globemaster - a large military transport aircraft is waiting for him on the tarmac, he knows it might be time again to test his mettle.

Chapter 5

The Fist of God

The Conference Room at the Mumbai Secretariat hummed with tension, a symphony of anxious whispers punctuated the occasional shuffle of papers. Seated at the head of the table are the bigwigs of the top security agencies, flanked by the Maharashtra Chief Minister and the ATS Chief. A lone laptop on a proxy chair represented the NSA-National Security Advisor. Amongst them is a boisterous bureaucrat, who clearly does not understand the seriousness of the situation and takes an incoming phone call "*Morya* ... *Morya*..... Happy Ganesh Chaturthi celebrations to you too...." He notices the glare of the Chief Minister, animatedly whispers into the phone and cuts the call. The focus once again shifts to Roma Thapa, who is debriefing the situation at hand.

The code "06 000 0.3 .7 000 .09 0.01.01 0.07" and the corresponding transcription, QUADATH-UT-ALLAH, is projected on a huge screen in the center of the conference room. Roma's commanding voice cuts through the murmurs. "A few hours ago, one of RAW's deep assets has provided us with a disturbing intel. "Roma speaks, pointing at the deciphered code. "And that is why we have convened this emergency meeting," Roma says, emphasizing the importance of the intel. Roma clicks a button, and the slide flips, showing the words "QADATH-UT-ALLAH = HAND OF GOD" "*Qadath -Ut-Allah* , literally means "Hand of God" ....But it also signifies, "Fist of God ", she makes a fist with her own hand to address the attendees. " It is a commonly used term in the Arab world, to describe an event, person or an act committed on the behalf of Allah, to avenge the atrocities on the Islamic world. "the bureaucrat whose mind is pre -occupied with the ongoing Ganesh Chaturthi preparations at his home continues to fiddle with his phone. He is getting fidgety, he interrupts, "This is an interesting story, but what is the connection here? Should we not be more concerned about our neighbours, Pakistan and especially China? Given the current circumstances," Munir Khan, who has been a silent observer so far , looks irritated *"Connection, hai sir,"* Munir interjects, rising from his seat to stand beside Roma. He lends weight to Roma's words and addresses the dignitaries. The various images of GULF WAR 1991- starts appearing on the screen. Amidst them are the pics of Saddam Hussain, with his troops making war plans. Munir's voice, tinged with authority, narrates the tale "It was 1991, a few months before the Gulf War. Saddam Hussain, was surrounded by American, British and the allied forces, but he had no plans to surrender, because he had a secret weapon - Project Babylon- also known as Qudath-Ut-Allah- meaning- Fist of God."

The bureaucrats' impatience continues, leading to yet another interruption. "What is our connection with Iraq now? Stop beating around the bush. As such, you have summoned us on the Ganesh Chaturthi holiday. Stop wasting our time and come to the point." A slight murmur is heard from the proxy chair of the NSA. Roma puts on the headphone and nods. "Sir, the NSA has asked you to leave the meeting. "She tells the bureaucrat. The bureaucrat babu tries to argue. Again, there is a murmur in Roma's headphone. She removes her headphone and puts the NSA on the speaker. "Congratulations, Mr. Kamble! You are now transferred to the Health Department of Jharkhand State as the Principal Secretary. We hope you will utilize your time there more effectively." Everyone, including Roma and Munir, exchange glances. The shocked bureaucrat exits murmuring under his breath, the meeting continues.

Munir elaborates on the current situation, using relevant slides, and then pauses briefly at the mention of two words: DHRUVA and CIRUS. "Based on the deciphered code - QUADATH -UT-ALLAH, we intercepted a few suspicious emails and found out, that two keywords seem to appear constantly in a cryptic form- DHRUVA and CIRUS. Besides being common names, Dhruva and Cirus, are also the names of the two nuclear reactors which make WAR-grade plutonium at BARC- Bhabha Atomic Research Centre, Mumbai." There is a deafening silence in the room. Munir chooses his next words carefully, "Fist of God- Quadath-Ut-Allah, was not just any secret weapon, it was a nuclear warhead believed to be developed by Saddam Hussain during the Gulf War."

Roma flicks the button again, a slide showing the image of the infamous Mushroom cloud, of the Hiroshima-Nagasaki explosion, comes up on the projector. The reflection of the destruction caused by nuclear weapons is clearly visible on the faces of dignitaries. Munir implies, "Our theory is that , the enemy is exploiting the situation in such a way that he can use our nuclear reactors , against us as nuclear bombs." Slides of Chernobyl and Fukushima disaster now get displayed on screen. "If the enemy is successful, then the situation in Mumbai could be much worse than Fukushima and Chernobyl. In one strike, the enemy would have wiped out the financial capital of India. India's economy will be on its knees, and we cannot even begin to estimate the loss of life , in Mumbai. "Munir presents an outcome from the situation. Most of the dignitaries , appear to be shaken by the very thought of such a probability becoming a reality, only the Defence Secretary retorts back. "How sure are you about this intel?" "Sir, in our line of work, you are never served the truth on a platter. Yes, there are always some facts, some theories, and some assumptions based on which we can gauge into the outcomes. We have to keep repeating , this cycle, keep digging at it, till we get to the core, and after we finally arrive at the truth, we have to avert such a thing from occurring in real time. "Munir remarks. Defence Secretary nods, exchanges a look with the ATS Chief in the room.

There is a murmur once again, in the proxy chair. Roma takes notice of it and asks Munir to take the call from NSA. "Jai Hind Sir" Munir greets in a respectable tone. NSA continues over the hotline. "Munir, I want you to look over the proceedings of this operation. Whatever clearances you need, I will make sure that they are on your table by tomorrow morning. Just get your A -Team on board and deal with this. And yes, "Drago" needs to be on this. "Munir, for the first time, looks uncomfortable. He argues, "Sir Drago is off the radar after that incident, and in any case we have a capable team to handle a situation such as this. "NSA counters back saying "Munir, there is no scope for error in this , Mumbai is at stake." Munir tries to press on, but the NSA cuts him short. "Look, Munir, Sahib, whatever differences you have, put it behind. "OPERATION MORYA", is bigger than anyone of us, our policy always has been Nation First. "The voice on the other end is stern yet reassuring, conveying the gravity of the situation and the urgency of action. Munir, is silent he gives in, with a response, "Yes sir". The NSA disconnects the phone with a formal salutation , "Jai Hind". Munir responds in the same currency- "Jai Hind".

With a sense of duty weighing heavily on his shoulders, Munir accepts the directive, knowing that the fate of millions rested in their hands. As the meeting adjourns, the room is abuzz with whispered conversations. One of the other bureaucrats in the room ,Mr Sharma the Head of NDRF (National Disaster Response Force) is inquiring with one of his subordinates, Mr Kamath- The Prinicipal Secretary of Public Relations Department. "Operation Morya–what kind of name is that ? In my time, I have known of Operation Black Tornado , spearheaded by NSG in the counter for Mumbai 2008 attacks, while Operation Trident , was during the 1971 War. " Mr Kamath, smiles "Morya is a Marathi word to express devotion and reverence towards Bhagwan Ganesha. People also revere Bhagwan Ganesha as Vighnaharta - the Lord who removes obstacles. Since this emergency has arisen during the time of Ganesha Chaturthi festivities, they might be calling it Operation Morya." Mr Sharma, the other bureaucrat, responds, even as he collects the files and folders from the table. "Who knows , Bappa might have a role to play in bringing a resolution. "Mr Kamath, has a worried expression on his face, as he responds to Mr Sharma. "If nuclear attack is a distinct possibility like the way Munir Sir explained, then we definitely need Bappa's blessings."

Munir and Roma happen to be overhearing this little banter between the two bureaucrats. Munir exchanges a knowing glance with Roma. It clearly is an uphill task, but their collective resolve seems unshaken by the challenges that lie ahead. With a silent nod, they both understand that the real battle has just begun - OPERATION MORYA, is officially underway.

Chapter 6

A Ghost Called -Drago

Roma and Munir are walking out through the busy corridor of the Mumbai Secretariat. Munir has a FAX in hand, while Roma is in the midst of an urgent conversation with Milind over the phone. "We need to know the details about that satellite signal vanishing in the Arabian embassy. Whoever carried that satellite phone could not have done it without someone assisting him from inside of the embassy. I need all the details." Milind updates her with the latest developments, "Yes, madam, we are on it. We are also digging into the records from the Russian Vessel, that ferried the suspect to Mumbai. I am hopeful once we zero in on the identity trails of the merchant navy crew, we will have some leads on this mysterious guy, "Roma acknowledges affirmatively, and disconnects the phone.

Munir has been in the waiting all this while , staring at the FAX detailing the whereabouts of DRAGO. He hands over the piece of paper to Roma, as she dives into the details, Munir speaks from his memory, looking at the wide expanse of the

Mumbai coastline visible from the building, "You will not find any AADHAR identification No. on him, nor a Driving License or a PAN Card by his name. His last known location is at an SBI Bank branch in Aarey Colony Goregaon (East), Mumbai, where he withdrew a sum of Rs 9,900 using a withdrawal slip, on 20 September, 2023. Roma finds it amusing, "So this Drago does not even have a debit card or a cheque book to his name". "No, not that we know of ". Munir shakes his head and continues. "This guy is technically a ghost and since the NSA wants him to be onboard for the mission...so" "What about you, sir? Do you want Drago on board or not?" Roma's tone holds a hint of inquiry. Munir hesitates. He struggles to articulate his thoughts. "I wish my answer was , as simple as your question. "Munir responds cryptically and his eyes fall on Roma's baby bump. He has an endearing smile. "5th month?" He inquires purposefully to avoid any further questions about Drago. Roma nods, Munir smiles back. He appears to be lost in his thoughts for a split second and then focuses again. "You trace down Drago...ok. I will look into , how Ministry of External Affairs can help us with the Arabian Embassy incident, although, I still think that,it is an isolated incident." Roma nods, acknowledging the complexities of their shared reality. Despite the uncertainty that looms over them, there is a sense of solidarity between them, a bond forged by their shared commitment for Operation Morya.

As Munir leaves, Roma watches him disappear down the corridor. A sense of determination settles over her being. She directs her mind towards tracking down Drago

Kochi, Kerala

24 September, 2023

1130 hrs

The tarmac of Kochi International Airport is abuzz with activity as the Emirates flight EK 530 from Dubai gracefully touches down and rolls to a halt at its designated gate. Inside the arrival lounge, anticipation crackles through the air , as families eagerly await their loved ones. The lounge resembles one big happy family of Malyalees, with their attires vibrantly showcasing their traditional wear—women adorned in white sarees with golden borders, and men sporting Mundus. Amidst them is an old lady, her kohl eyes , and henna coated hair hinting at her identity. Her eyes dance with excitement as she scans the incoming crowd, searching for a familiar face.

From the speakers overhead, the flight announcer's voice resonates in Malayalam, announcing the arrival of the flight and directing passengers to collect their luggage. The scene unfolds with passengers shuffling towards the immigration counter. The government officials diligently scrutinize the passports, ensuring smooth transitions for the travellers.

One such traveller, Sadiq, stands before the Immigration Officer, his anticipation is palpable. "It's a Student Visa, sir, returning from Dubai University. I am here for the Onam holidays," he affirms confidently, his thoughts already drifting to the upcoming Onam celebrations, his return home for the festive season. The officer looks at the passport, and then back at the face of Sadiq. He is the same guy who had shot the Indian Agent in ISIS territory of Mosul, Syria. A brisk stamp on the passport follows. Sadiq breathes a sigh of relief. He looks at the other immigration counters, as if he is looking for someone. As he moves towards the exit, his two accomplices join him. It is the same trio who had done significant damage to the Indian mission in ISIS territory. Skilfully blending into the crowd, they conceal their past actions behind the facade of ordinary travellers. They seamlessly merge with the throng of passengers and proceed to reunite with their respective families.

Outside, in the joyous chaos of reunions, Sadiq finally spots his mother. Ameena, the old lady with kohl eyes, and henna colored hair. With a heart full of emotion, Sadiq approaches her, performing the traditional tasleem as a sign of respect. "*Karthika nahin aayi*?" he inquires eagerly, his eyes searching.

His mother's toothless smile holds a world of emotions as she replies, "*Beta*, she is waiting for you in Bombay!" In her appreciative gaze is a tale of longing and separation, a reminder that even amidst the joy of homecoming, some reunions remain deferred, awaiting their own time to unfold.

RAW Headquarters, Mumbai

24 September, 2023

1200 hrs

Roma is at the command centre with all the CCTV cameras and modern surveillance technology, integrated with Geo Tagging, at her disposal. Roma and her analysts are working diligently to track down the whereabouts of Drago, currently they appear to be busy collating intel from different sources like traffic cameras, face recognition tech and feeding that into the electronic main frame, which they call as IIS- Integrated Intelligence System. Various images pulled from the CCTV network keep shuffling on the main screen. A small digital sandbox in the right-hand bottom corner of the screen shows a data trail. Just by the side of the mainframe is a small screen on the side to assist the operators, with the geographical positioning in what appears to be the DIGITAL TWIN of the Mumbai city.

Munir, walks in with a cup of hot Adrakh wali chai, in his hands. Roma quickly acknowledges his presence and walks up to him referring to some notes, she has been scribbling on her notepad. Roma signals the operator of the IIS- Integrated Intelligence System to pull up the previous frame. The CCTV grab comes alive on the big screen. A tall man wearing a cap appears on the main screen. The time stamp on the screen suggests it is footage from that morning at 9:03 AM near Byculla crossing.

Roma turns to address Munir once again, "Your guy Drago is indeed difficult to track. It's as if this guy knows exactly where each CCTV camera is installed. "Munir responds with a cold demeanour," Ya, what can I say? This one likes to stay under the radar. He's unpredictable, follows his gut, and sometimes even throws the rulebook out of the window. But when faced with challenges and overwhelming odds, he often steps up and rises to the occasion. A word of caution though, he has no regard for the life of the people around him and neither for his own. "Roma cannot understand , if it is Munir's admiration for the man or a grudge he holds against him. She side steps from her thoughts and points to the CCTV grab of Drago. "Sir, this is from this morning, 0903 hrs, but we could not trace him any further." Munir has a closer look at the grab, he nods, "That looks like him, reverse the footage by a few seconds and playback. "The operator does as instructed and the footage plays once again. Munir suddenly instructs to freeze frame once again. "What is he carrying in his hands?" The operator zooms on to the side profile of Drago. He appears to be carrying an animal. Everyone, including Roma, focuses on the screen. Roma, "It looks like a cat?" Munir cuts her off. "He loves animals, but this has to be a dog. Replay the footage from a little before. The operator does as instructed, playing the footage from a few more seconds from before, where Drago appears to pick up the dog, the dog seems to have a bit of a limp. Munir orders to go back to the frame where they had lost track of Drago. Roma helps the controller to identify the frame. "Please flag up all the available Geo tags of surrounding area." Munir instructs. The operator punches in a few commands, and the screen displays a multitude of Geo-tags. Munir has his eyes locked on the screen. Roma and her colleagues segregate the Geo tags into categories, even as Munir continues to scrutinize." We should look here… "Munir remarks, pointing at the tag of Bombay Veterinary Clinic. The operator zooms onto the Geo Tag , of Bombay Veterinary Clinic, revealing its complete address in the Byculla area. Roma intervenes, "How can you be so sure?" "Do you remember those Vodafone ads, where a dog follows the man everywhere? "Roma recollects the famous Vodafone commercial in her head. She nods. "It's exactly the other way round in this case. You follow the dog, and you will get to the man." At that moment, Munir turns around and starts walking away. He notices Roma is not around. "Roma , aren't you coming? "Munir retorts. Roma fumbles as she responds assertively. Roma still does not get the complete logic of Munir's statement, but she realizes in the same breath that Munir must have known Drago closely.

Serene music appears to play in the background. A man in his early 30s appears with his eyes closed. Then a distant sound reaches Drago's ears, "Mr. Dheeraj, Mr. Dheeraj." Dheeraj opens his eyes, the psychedelic music pouring into his ears from his air pods is in contrast to this upside-down world view of his. He's in a Shirsasana pose. A cute young boy with round glasses stares at him, his cocker spaniel equally intrigued with Dheeraj's upside-down pose, while a lady veterinarian stands nearby, calling out for Dheeraj.

Dheeraj Singh, gradually unwinds his pose, the cocker spaniel bends his neck sideways, to figure out how this man stood upside down. "Sorry *wohh...Shirsasan...*" explains Dheeraj; the young boy and the dog exchange a glance, silently acknowledging the yoga pose. The doctor seems uninterested in Dheeraj's explanation. "Any pose would do. I'm just here to inform you that your dog's surgery was successful. He'll need to be kept under observation for 48 hours, then you can take him home." The Veterinarian walks away, even without acknowledging Dheeraj's gratitude. Dheeraj appears unaffected, his wide frame turns the other way round to notice the cute boy with round glasses and his cocker spaniel still staring at him. The young boy takes out his phone and speaks, "Hello Google, what is Shirsasan? "The google assistant unravels a well-rehearsed, pre -recorded information capsule on Shirsasan. Dheeraj meanwhile , lowers himself to the child's level, he prods, "Google will tell you everything about the yoga pose, and its benefits, but it will not tell you that, the yoga pose is also known as, "Utt-Patang Aasan" The boy gets excited, "No way ....Utt Patang Aasan, that is like the coolest thing I have heard today" Dheeraj puts his hands out, the boy gives him a Hi-five , the cocker spaniel also whispers with a bit of huff and puff. "You must try it sometime. It gives you such an upside-down view of the world , that you see things more clearly. "Just then, a voice from afar interrupts their exchange, casting a shadow of curiosity over the conversation." And sometimes even a whole new perspective about the world may not be enough, isn't it! Drago." Munir's voice resonates through the room, accompanied by Roma's silent presence.

"Drago", only a selected few people, called Dheeraj by that name. He looks on, notices Munir in the distance, and acknowledges Munir's words. He nods solemnly. "*Sahi kaha apne*. Sometimes, even a whole new perspective might fall short. What truly matters, though, is only the result." Drago and Munir are locked in a stare for a few moments. Some painful memories from the past resurface on their faces. The search for the questions that were never asked and the answers that were never given continue to reflect in their body language. Roma observes their silent exchange, from the vantage point, she is still figuring out the equation between the two, even as her thoughts drift into the realm of the trio's intertwined destinies, which had brought them together for their currently assigned mission- OPERATION MORYA.

Chapter 7

The Name Is Nicolas...

Nicolas's trip to Mumbai in September 2022 was one of his most vibrant experiences. An avid traveller and a documentary filmmaker from France, he had heard about Ganpati-The Elephant Headed God, even seen his pictures and sculptures. However, it was only on his previous visit to Mumbai that he truly absorbed the beauty and significance of the Ganesha Chaturthi festivities. The thousands of Ganesha idols, which people brought home in the lord's reverence, the little rituals leading to Pran Pratishthapana, the delicious Modaks, countless stories, throngs of people waiting in queues to take darshan, at different pandals. Nicolas remembered everything, like it had happened yesterday. The various stories of Ganpati Bappa fascinated him. The tale that intrigued him the most was how Ganesha gained the title Vighnaharta - The Destroyer of All Obstacles. What really captivated him, however, was the Visarjan ceremony. Unsure if it was the sea of devotion or the grand celebrations, he decided to come back next year and film the complete Ganesha Chaturthi festivities.

24 September, 2023
2000 hrs

As he made his way out from the Terminal 2 of the Chattrapati Shivaji International Airport at Mumbai tonight, he could already feel the festive vibe in the air. The airport management was also busy preparing for Ganpati Bappa's arrival at the designated space near the arrival lounge.Nicolas exits the lounge and scans the bustling crowd. Amidst the sea of people holding placards for their respective guests, one placard catches his attention—it bears his name: "Nicolas Forget." He approaches the placard and is greeted by Ovaise Sheikh- The man who had disappeared inside the Arabian Embassy, had resurfaced again. This time he was not hiding from anyone, in fact just a few moments earlier, he had borrowed a match stick from a CRPF Airport Security Personnel to light his cigarette, he thanked the security personnel, flashing his broad grin and parted ways with a salutation, "*Ganpati Bappa Morya.*"

Ovaise warmly extends a welcome in French. Surprised by the gesture, Nicolas responds in English, mixed with French. "*Merci Merci...* But I can speak English," he said with a hint of amusement in his tone.

"*Tres Bien Merci.* I was just polishing my French. As a production support executive for your documentary team, this is the least I can do," Ovaise replies with a smile, effortlessly transitioning from French to English, he takes control of Nicolas's luggage, and leads the way towards their car. "Hope your work is as good as your French. As you already know, we are on a tight schedule, and I would like to check our shooting equipment first," Nicolas remarks, his tone businesslike yet cordial.

"*Oui,* sir. This way, please," Ovaise responds, his demeanour professional as they get in the car..

Ovaise takes the wheel and as they exit the airport, they drive past the beautifully adorned Ganesha Pandals along the roadside. Mumbai, the city itself, appears to be vibrant and full of zest. With each passing mile in the Mumbai traffic, the scene gets set for unexpected encounters and challenges that lay ahead of both these men, each one on a mission of his own making.

Chapter 8

Caught In The Crossfire

Drago sits at the messy desk, tracing his fingers over the transcribed code Quadath-Ut-Allah and its corresponding original "06 000 0.3 .7 000 .09 0.01.01 0.07". He flips through the BARC file, with two booklets "Cirus" and "Dhruva" kept on the side. Roma watches him as he continues flipping through the files; her own attention nervously shifting to her associates, Milind, Munir and the Commissioner of Police seated on the other side of the round table in Police Commissioner of Mumbai's office. "Any potential suspects?" Drago asked, breaking the heavy silence that hung in the air. Roma ruffles through the files until she finds what she was looking for—a photograph sent by the RAW agent in Syria. She passes it to Drago. It is the picture of Sadiq and his two accomplices. "Share these pictures with all the international airports of our country. Scan and collate all the incoming traffic data from two days prior to the day you have received this intel. That will be 21 September onwards." Drago advises. Milind quickly takes notes. Roma nods and Drago continues to scan through the files with his eagle eyes.

"Sir, we will need all the support and human intelligence you can provide," Roma shifts her attention, addressing the Police Commissioner seated nearby. The Commissioner nods solemnly. " We fully support you, but you will also have to cut us some slack. Most of our force is busy with the security vigil for the Ganesh Chaturthi celebration and, for BARC related matters, depend on CISF, because it comes under their jurisdiction. "Munir interjects, "Sir, this is officially a Level 3 alert. We all will have to go above and beyond our abilities to counter it," The Commissioner reassures them, acknowledging the delicate balance between addressing the threat and managing the security situation. " I am not taking it lightly. I am just giving you a realistic view." He adds," The Maharashtra State Elections are also around the corner. There are some rallies scheduled in the coming days, and one of them will be addressed by the Prime Minister. "

The Commissioner and his entourage get up from their table, signalling an end to their brief meet up. Drago has more darting insights to share, but unfortunately, he is also forced to get up. However, he inquires a bit more about PM's rally. "Yes, he is inaugurating a new metro station near Bandra Kurla Complex, and with state elections around the corner, you know how it will get positioned, right! "The commissioner concludes the meeting with a touch of sarcasm and adds," ACP Sarnaik, will be your point of contact for Operation Morya. Let me see what else can I do for you guys. Jai Hind." Munir responds with the same salutation, while Roma and Milind prepare to leave with the files.

Drago realizes the meeting was a mere formality. He shoots a glance at Munir. Having worked alongside Munir in the past, he realized Munir also wanted more from the meeting with the Commissioner of Police.

Roma interjects, addressing Drago, “Sir, there is one more thing - we traced a non-descript signal from an incoming merchant navy vessel at JNPT dock recently.” The Coast Guard chased the satellite signal, but it went dark around the Arabian Embassy. “Munir opines, “Roma, I agree this is an unusual incident, but it has nothing to do with the BARC security threat. ““Sir, I agree, they may not look related right now, but , there might be a connection. There is no harm in exploring. “Roma responds. Drago, who has been listening, weighs in with his opinion. “Munir, Sir, I think there is no harm in pursuing the lead. As soldiers, we’ve learned that there’s always more than meets the eye, and sometimes trusting our instincts is more important than our actions on the battlefield.” At first, Munir appears hesitant. Then he realizes that he has to take this matter up with the Arabian Embassy, in any case, so he might as well prioritize it. He looks at Roma and then shifts his gaze to Drago. “Ok Roma, we will go with your instincts. I will fast track the matter with the Home Ministry. “Drago continues to look at Munir and responds, “Good job , Roma!” and then he shifts his glance to meet Roma’s eyes with a smile. Roma smiles back, evidently she also realizes the tension between the two.

Western Express Highway, Mumbai

24 September, 2023

2030 hrs

Ovaise is driving through the Mumbai roads. He eventually gets stuck in Mumbai’s office hour crawl, but Nicolas isn’t complaining, as he gets the best views of the Bappa’s temporary abodes on the way. The traffic is so slow that a young boy appears to be walking faster amidst the cars , on the Western Expressway. Apparently, he is selling roasted peanuts to people stuck in traffic. It was this paradox , that attracted Nicolas , to this maximum city. Nicolas buys a pack of Peanuts in exchange of a 10 Rs. note and cheers "*Ganpati Bappa Morya*" The boy finds it weird, a smile erupts on his face, and then he walks away to the next car, his next potential customer.

Nicolas offers the cone of roasted peanuts to Ovaise, which he politely declines. "What is the number of Ganesha idols that Mumbai will host this year?" Nicolas asks, his curiosity piqued. Ovaise promptly answers, "Sir, this year we have around 8000 public installations, such as the Saravajanik Ganpati Mandals, and about 190,000 idols at people's homes." Nicolas marvels at the magnitude of festivities. "Wow, that is significantly more than last year. I have a good feeling about this documentary." The traffic signal in the distance turns green, and the traffic now moves more swiftly than before.

Their car eventually comes to a halt outside a nondescript godown on an arterial road of Goregaon (East). Nicolas looks around the area. A few industrial shades appear to be lined up in a row. "Are we at the correct address? " Nicolas appears puzzled. "Everything has been arranged, sir. You will see it for yourself," Ovaise assures Nicolas. The light equipment godown stood silent under the soft light of the waxing moon. Ovaise ushered Nicolas through the entrance of the nondescript gala in the industrial area, the weight of uncertainty settling upon them both. "The team is waiting for you inside, sir," Ovaise announces as they step into the cavernous space. Workers greet Nicolas with nods and murmured acknowledgments. Nicolas notices, that the godown is buzzing with activity—a red-colored water tanker is being painted in one corner, a makeshift office setup is being manned by a geek-looking individual, whereas a meticulously crafted Ganapati Idol is visible in another corner.

"Here, sir. This is the Ganesha Idol you requested. We would use it for close-up shots with the host, "Ovaise explains. Nicolas inspects the idol. It appears impressive. Next to it, two men work diligently on a small replica of a fighter jet, featuring a lifelike sculpture of a fighter pilot standing beside it. "What is this?" Nicolas questions. "Sir, this is a surprise addition from the TV Channels production designer. She wanted to include this in the narrative of one of the Ganpati Pandal décor exhibits. "Ovaise realizes his explanation is not convincing. "Sir, this is in the memory of India's victorious air strike in Balakot, Pakistan. This fighter pilot was a hero of that dogfight, in which he brought down , a much superior F-16 fighter jet with his MIG-21. He is Wing Commander Abhinandan Varthman, look at this handle bar moustache, doesn't it look real" Ovaise glances at his geeky accomplice standing nearby. They know , they cannot put up with the façade any longer.

Nicolas nods and moves along, but amidst the semblance of normalcy, something feels amiss to him. His eyes fall upon the scattered light equipment in the centre of the space, prompting him to retrieve the light equipment requirement list from his pocket and verify. Most equipment is present, but some specific lights he had mentioned are missing. "This is not everything that I had asked for!" Nicolas exclaims, his voice tinged with dissatisfaction as he turns to address Ovaise.

Before any more words could escape his lips, a sound echoes from the front door. Nicolas turns to see a man closing the main door. Panic sets in as he realizes he had walked into a trap, but before he can react, powerful hands seize him from behind.The three men from the ISIS photograph emerge from the shadows, their faces now twisted with menace. They waste no time in overpowering Nicolas. His protests are met with brute force, and his hands are forcefully bound behind his back.

Riaz, the geek-looking figure, steps forward. A predatory gleam is apparent in his eyes ,as he confiscates Nicolas's passport and begins scanning it. Nicolas struggles against his restraints, only to be met with a stinging slap from Sadiq.

Undeterred, Nicolas continues to resist. His defiance meets with escalating violence. With a chilling calmness, Riaz produces a gun, the metallic glint sending a shiver down Nicolas's spine. Before he can comprehend the full extent of the danger, a gunshot pierces the air, and agony sears through Nicolas's foot.

Nicolas winces in pain. One aide brings a chair and sets it up. Right opposite Nicolas, Ovaise takes his seat, and sits with his legs folded, like a spectator watching an opera unfold in front of his eyes. The geeky lad Riaz clicks a picture of Ovaise, with an instant camera and immediately rushes back to his workstation. A special facial reconstruction software promptly opens up, it compares Nicolas and Ovaise's faces and starts matching the facial points to prepare a fresh crew id for Ovaise. He gives the final touches, with the software, to make Ovaise's picture look as similar to Nicolas as possible. Riaz takes the final print of the CREW ID, with his name now mentioned as Nicolas Forget, he hands over the CREW ID to Ovaise, who looks impressed with the work. Riaz does not stop to acknowledge even, as he walks over to Nicolas, takes his phone and dials his wife's number. Nicolas watches the phone screen in horror as his wife's mobile number starts ringing. "Tell her you have landed in India. You're fine and will be occupied with work for the next 2-3 days. You will call when you can, " Riaz instructs. Nicolas looks terrified, but he desperately wants to get back to Riaz. Riaz reads his mind and puts a gun to his head. " *Aee Dedh shahne, chadi mein rehneka*! You know my boss knows how to speak French. *Oui*." Nicolas , looks at Ovaise sitting right in front of him, his eyes are filled with malice. Nicolas's wife's voice comes alive from the other side of the phone. Riaz cocks the gun , Nicolas has to make a quick decision. "*Oui*", Nicolas , submissively says , he nods looking at Riaz and Ovaise. He informs his wife, dropping no hints. Ensnared in a trap, the real Nicolas could only brace himself for the unknown horrors that lay ahead.

Ovaise observes Nicolas keenly, "*Merci Monsieur, Vous me remercierez plus tard*." He walks away to the workstation, where his laptop is already placed. He types in his password, to access the system and inserts a movie DVD of Bajirao Mastani , the background music of the film starts playing, he focusses intently on the screen.

Chapter 9

The Threat is Real...

25 September, 2023
0900 hrs

BARC - Bhabha Atomic Research Centre, named after the Father of India's Nuclear Programme, Dr. Homi Bhabha , BARC is nestled in the heart of Mumbai. Unlike the hustle and bustle of the maximum city, where India's financial centre thrives, BARC stands as a beacon of scientific prowess and technological innovation. Its sprawling campus, flanked by the serene waters of the sea and embraced by the rugged silhouette of mountains, exudes an air of both grandeur and secrecy. Within its confines, research and development initiatives unfold, shaping the future of nuclear technology in India. Guarded vigilantly by the CISF-Central Industrial Security Force, its entry and exit points echo with the hum of activity, that lie within its formidable walls.

As Drago stood at the vantage point of BARC, surrounded by the endless expanse of the sea on one side and the towering mountains on the other, he couldn't shake the unease, that settled within him. Milind meanwhile, had been taking pictures of the BARC, and making his own notes for reference. The BARC , scientist S Ramnathan ,was talking to his senior on the phone, but it was the cigarette smoke billowing from the BARC scientist's lips which added to Drago's discomfort.

"Sir, cigarette smoking is injurious to health," Drago remarks, as soon as ,Ramnathan gets off the phone, his voice tinged with concern.

The scientist, seemingly unperturbed, waves off Drago's comment. "Never mind sir, we have more pressing issues to attend to first."

With a resigned sigh, Drago follows the scientist on a brief tour of the BARC Campus, and Milind also tags along. Despite the scientist's incessant smoking, he speaks with fervour about the institution's research endeavours. He opens a blueprint of the map on his tablet computer, demarking the various entry , exit gates/ points at the BARC and broadly defines the different reactors built within the campus. "BARC conducts research on every aspect of nuclear technology for India, and it is one of the premium most research institutes on nuclear physics across the world " Ramnathan, explains punctuating his words with puffs of smoke.

As they navigate through the campus, Drago's attention is drawn to a space, that resembles a dumpsite. But before he could voice his curiosity, the scientist gestures for him to continue onward. Milind also notices this but with Drago , not raising a voice , he also has little choice, but to move along.

"Although most of the research projects in BARC are inclined towards civil application, most people don't know ,that BARC also produces, 90% of India's weapon grade Plutonium. BARC was also responsible for producing the nuclear fuel used in the Pokhran Nuclear Tests," the scientist added, his tone assuming a matter-of-fact manner.

Ramnathan finally, leads them on to "Dhruva" and "Cirus" the crown jewels of BARC. Drago scrutinizes them with keen interest, his mind abuzz with questions.

"What can you tell me about the safety systems of these reactors ?" Drago inquires, his gaze unwavering. The scientist, now animated by Drago's interest, begins to elaborate on the intricate safety measures in place within the reactors. " Sir these reactors have tough containment systems, integrated into it during the time of construction itself." As Ramnathan speaks, Drago finds himself immersed in the intricacies of nuclear technology, his initial apprehension gives way to fascination.

"To be frank, only a specially air-delivered bomb or missile could cause any damage to these reactors," the scientist concludes; his words hanging heavy in the air. As Drago absorbs this observation, he gives a long hard look at the scientist.

A few minutes later, top dignitaries including Munir, Roma , CISF Chief at BARC and BARC scientists are seated. Drago , gestures the scientist to speak. Milind , meanwhile is putting some papers in order and setting up the photos , he had previously clicked at the site. And by his side is a strange looking aluminium can.

Ramnathan seems a little anxious as he speaks to the motely group in the small conference hall at the BARC. "Sir, after analysing various probabilities, regarding the security parameters of the BARC facility, I have arrived at the conclusion , that Dhruva and Cirus reactors, can only explode in an extraordinary event like an air bomb or missile attack. "

Drago interjects purposefully," He is telling the truth, but only a dumb ass, will think of taking this aerial route or missile strike, as a plausible way to launch an attack on India's nuclear facility. Infact let me give you a small demo to explain how it can be actually done. "

Everybody in the room looks confused. Drago, signals Milind, who hands over a jerry can to him. Drago places this completely filled jerry can on the table and rotates it around for everyone to see the word "PETROL " written on it in bold letters. " Think of this jerry can as a Petrol Pump. " Drago asks everyone to spark their imagination.

Drago, then forcibly , borrows the lighter from Ramnathan. He returns to the jerry can and starts triggering the lighter to check if it is working fine , to put jerry can on fire. The scientist looks worried. " To blow up the petrol pump , I don't need to attack the petrol pump." Drago continues with his discourse and spills some of the liquid from the jerry can , on the table to make a long trail of the liquid. Everybody in the room appears to be resentful as Drago lights up the lighter and takes it near the liquid spilled over the table. " If I light up this spillage, it will automatically start spreading, it will reach the petrol pump in a matter of seconds and boom ." Drago dramatically explains. Ramnathan is shaken up by now, " This is an atrocious way to explain , and this guy is very dangerous, what if this fuel would have really caught fire. " Drago cuts him off , " Relax it will not catch fire. It is water. " He takes a sip of water from the jerry can , to wet his throat. He then walks up to the scientist and places the lighter back in his pocket , Drago states, " I asked them to write , the word. Petrol , I was only trying to make a point. "

On his way back to the presentation dias he signals Milind to flick on his laptop, and the image of BARC's blueprint comes alive on the projected screen. " If anyone has to blow up BARC , he will not launch a direct attack on 'DHRUV" or " CIRUS". He will attack here . " Drago marks the spent nuclear fuel dumpsite on the BARC Campus. A worried expression emerges on the face of the scientist Ramnathan, he recollects the moments from their brief tour of the BARC , when Drago had insisted to go back to the dumpsite.

Drago's mind was still stuck on the open site they had come across , Drago asks the scientist to take him back to dumpsite, Ramnathan is reluctant , Drago pre-empt's his thoughts and put his foot down, " If you are not going to take us there , I will make sure that your boss sends someone else." Drago resonates his authority, and gestures Milind to make a call, Milind is about to make a call, when Ramnathan , agrees to fall in line and takes them back to the dumpsite.

Milind takes a few pictures of the well protected but open to air dumpsite, infront of them. "Can you explain what is all this?" Drago's voice cuts through the silence, his tone laced with disbelief as he gestures towards the array of barrels containing spent nuclear fuel. Ramnathan's gaze flickering uneasily before finally meeting Drago's probing stare. "That's the spent nuclear fuel site," he explains, his words tinged with apprehension. "Why are there no security cameras here? Not even manual surveillance here ?" Drago demands, his voice edged with impatience.

Ramnathan holds his nerve as he explains, " Sir technically this is spent nuclear fuel, it is of no use to us. It is meant to be systematically disposed off to another site far away from here. The waste is accumulated here and then once it becomes a sizeable quantity , protocols are followed to dispose it off. "

Drago is not satisfied by the scientist's explanation. "Despite being nuclear waste, the material is still radioactive, correct?", Drago's tone is sharper now. The scientist hesitates for a moment before nodding reluctantly. "Yes, sir, but you're missing the point," he murmurs, his voice barely audible above the gentle rustle of the wind. But Drago is not the one to be deterred. His mind races with the possibilities, each one more ominous ,than the last.

Ramnathan's reverie breaks , as Milind places the report of IAEA- International Atomic Energy Association amongst the dignitaries in the conference room. Drago addresses the panel , " According to this independent report by IAEA this spent nuclear fuel , is more radioactive then reactor cores. A blast of reasonable magnitude can trigger radioactivity here and the fire will spread to Dhruv and Cirus reactors in no time. And one of the outcomes could be nuclear annihilation." Drago emphasise on the word nuclear annhilation to drive his point home.

As the tense atmosphere lingers in the conference room, the implications of Drago's demonstration begins to sink in. Munir, Roma, the CISF Chief, and the BARC scientists exchange concerned glances, their minds grappling with the gravity of the situation. Drago's methods were unorthodox, but they were always backed by strong reasoning , and it had a way of cutting through the fog of complacency. Yet again, Drago, had managed to present his point with stealth. It was this quality of Drago , that Munir had always admired, and he had also seen the physical manifestation of the same on the battle field.

Munir clears his throat, breaking the heavy silence that enveloped the room. He began, his voice steady despite the turmoil within. "Drago may be unconventional, but his methods have revealed that—we are vulnerable."

Roma nods in agreement, her expression resolute. "We need to reassess our security protocols," she asserted, her gaze sweeping across the gathered assembly. "We cannot allow ourselves to be caught off guard again."

The CISF Chief, his features etched with concern, spoke up next. "We must strengthen our defences, and put new protocols in place " he urged, his tone decisive. "Every possible measure will be taken to safeguard the facility."

Outside the confines of the meeting room, the corridors of BARC buzzed with whispered conversations and hurried footsteps. The news of Drago's demonstration spread like wildfire, sending ripples of anxiety through the facility's staff. It was evident, that their sense of security had been replaced by a spectre of uncertainty.

Chapter 10

Murugan Chawl – The Trap of Belief

25 September 2023

1830 hrs

Standing against the setting sun, Murugan Chawl, stood as a testament to the resilience of its inhabitants. A sprawling tangle of narrow alleys and crumbling buildings nestled within the heart of Khar-Bandra in Suburban Mumbai. The chawl appeared as a maze of interconnected structures, each bearing the scars of time and neglect. As one ventured deeper, the true character of Murugan Chawl revealed itself—a microcosm of urban life teeming with a vibrant tapestry of what they call as - The Bombay Life. The streets bustled with activity, alive with the hustle and bustle of daily life. Vendors peddled their wares along the crowded sidewalks, their makeshift stalls overflowing with a kaleidoscope of colors and scents. Community bonds ran deep within the chawl, weaving a tight-knit fabric of solidarity and support that held its residents together in times of need. For many, Murugan Chawl, was not just a place to live, but a sanctuary—a refuge from the harsh realities of the outside world.

As the sun started descending below the horizon, Sadiq navigated the crowded street with practiced ease. He passed by makeshift stalls and dilapidated shanties, exchanging Tasleem with familiar faces. A couple of old ladies who are selling some home grown weed to a couple of rich looking college kids, acknowledge his presence with fleeting smiles. Sadiq comes across an old accomplice, Fajeesh, who is sauntering around with his young son, "*Aree Sadiq Cheta*!!". He introduces Sadiq to his son with a tone of aspiration."Look, son, this is Sadiq Miyaan. He is a man of Allah. Walk on the path of Allah, like he does, and Allah will bless you with abundance as well." Sadiq gracefully responds, "*Alhamdulillah*!" and proceeds to a nondescript building tucked away in a corner of the slum—Here amidst the squalor of decay , Sadiq finds solace in the familiar embrace of his home.

Upon entering, his mother greets him; her weathered face adorned with a toothless smile. With a silent gesture, Sadiq inquires about her well-being, his eyes scanning the room in search of his better half. Sadiq's mother points toward backyard. In the backyard, bathed in the soft glow of the sun, stood a woman facing the west, her fingers tracing the prayer beads in her hands. Sadiq approaches her silently and tries holding her from behind. The woman feels scared. *"Fatima, meri jaan, mein hoon,"* he murmurs softly, his voice a gentle reassurance amidst the turmoil.

He unfurls a vibrant fuchsia coloured scarf over her head, a faint smile tugs at the corners of Sadiq's lips. "*Subhanallah,* I knew this color would suit you," he remarks. But Fatima's thoughts are elsewhere, her mind consumed by a single question. "Where is Rizwan?" she pleads, her voice tinged with desperation. "You are seeing your husband after such a long time, yet the only thing that concerns you is your kid." Sadiq's expression hardens, Fatima, retaliates. Sadiq forcefully holds her down and shows her the latest picture of Rizwan. He is having fun in what appears to be a play zone in Dubai. Fatima, takes the mobile and zooms to have a closer look at her son. "Everything is fine and it will remain that way, but if you will stop cooperating with them, then first our son will bear the consequences and then you," Sadiq declares, his tone laced with an underlying threat. Fatima remains unmoved, her eyes brimming with tears as she clutches the mobile phone with her son's picture closer to her chest. Sadiq emphatically wipes her tears. "Fatima, you are my wife. Why will I make you do anything wrong? Infact, you should be thankful that we showed you the path towards one true God. "Sadiq implores, his voice tinged with a hint of desperation. "*Meri baat samjhne ki koshish karo begum, shahid kabhi marte nahin , woh toh jannat ki sair karte hai.*"

As he strokes her head tenderly, a shadow of fear flickers in Fatima's eyes—a silent acknowledgment of the truth that lay hidden beneath the familial love. She wonders, how can Sadiq be so blinded by his faith that he cannot even see his own ruin at the end of the road. As the sun dipped below the horizon, casting long shadows across the barren landscape of Murugan Chawl, Fatima knew that the time of judgement is upon her, and no matter what she chooses, she will be on the losing side.

CHAPTER 11
Connecting the Dots...

BARC Campus, Mumbai

26 September, 2023
0700 Hrs

Security measures at BARC were ramped up to unprecedented levels. Guards patrolled the perimeter with heightened vigilance, and access to sensitive areas was restricted even further. A sense of unease lingered in the air at BARC, a silent reminder of the lurking danger that Drago had so effectively unveiled.

The conference room at BARC hummed with the energy of urgency. What once was a space for deliberation and planning on matters related to nuclear physics, now stood transformed into a war room, alive with the frenetic activity of RAW Analysts pouring over screens, and dissecting data with determined focus.

Munir, a picture of intensity, engaged in an animated conversation with the CISF Chief. Before them, the map of

BARC lay sprawled, a canvas upon which they meticulously sketched out a new protocol of security measures.

Drago poured over blueprints and schematics, his mind consumed by the task at hand. With each passing moment, the weight of responsibility bore down upon him, driving him to push the boundaries of conventional thinking in search of a solution, yet he was well aware of his surroundings.

He was well aware of, Roma juggling personal and professional matters effortlessly. Milind, her steadfast companion, diligently compiled crucial data, his concentration unwavering amidst the chaos. Roma was multitasking, as she negotiated appointments and assurances over the phone." Naah , I won't be able to make it to the Aarti . I had to even reschedule my appointment with the Gynaecologist. " Roma instructs Milind in signs , as she continues to listen on the phone and resumes her conversation, rolling her eyes. " Yaa ,yaa, I will figure out the Gynaec appointment for tomorrow. *Acha suno naa,* please offer prayers on my behalf and the one who is about to come into our little world. And listen don't forget to get the *modak prasad*.... ok love you......"

Roma, hangs up the phone to notice the scientist Ramnathan, grinning at her. Seated next to him is Drago, who is working on the computer, the photograph of 3 suspects sent by the RAW Agent from Syria is currently open on his screen. " You have such a loving and caring husband. " even as Ramnathan compliments Roma, Drago, whispers softly shaking his head, "Roma is not married..." Roma counters with a smile, "He is not my husband. " The scientist is embarrassed, he looks sideways and inquires with Drago in a hushed tone. " You said, you met these guys just a few hours earlier , then how do you know such intricate details.

" Drago, signals him to come closer. " I even know ,that you were not giving her a genuine compliment ." Ramnathan's face goes white, "Earlier, I put you in a tight spot in front of everyone, and now you are doing everything you can, to take corrective measures and make a good impression on us. And I personally think, whatever you are doing is justified." Ramnathan, feels even more abashed.

From Drago's POV , Munir is visibly in a discussion with CISF Chief but he has been constantly looking at his watch. " I also know that Munir sir is making new security plans with the CISF officer but in reality he is wondering , why has he still not got an update from the Arabian Embassy. "

Drago taps on Ramnathan's shoulder and draws his attention towards Milind, who is going through the data of different employee profiles. The excitement of a new finding is apparent on his face. " Milind , thinks he has stumbled upon something from the records which will be a breakthrough in the current investigation. And Milind will be calling me to share this info in the next 5 seconds…."

The scientist is both amazed and confused, as he stares at Drago, who counts down from 5,4,3,2,1. " Dheeraj sir you need to have a look at this ?" Milind addresses Drago with a tone of excitement. Drago nods and gestures Milind to come to his desk. Ramnathan watches on amused, as Milind , carries his laptop, and walks towards Drago with a few printouts in his hands. Drago, signals Roma and Munir to join in. Milind places a few employee profiles on the table. " Sir we have been tracking a few employee ID's " Milind hands, over the details of some employee ID's. " Amongst all these ID's, Karthika Nair's case is peculiar." Milind points at the ID he has marked on the list , and then switches on the laptop screen.

" Karthika , has been on LWP -Leave Without Pay for last 3 months. The residential quarters allotted by BARC, has been locked for a time, longer than that. On inquiring with the neighbours we learnt that , Karthika , has gone to her village in Kerala. " The photo of Karthika pops up on screen, with a detailed investigation trail , mentioned in the analysis. Milind awaits some reaction from his seniors.

Roma, the strategist, wastes no time in mobilizing their resources, dispatching inquiries to local authorities and digging deeper into Karthika's past. "Get in touch with the Chembur Police Station ...I need all the facts and fiction related to the life of this girl, also get her phone tracked. Drago weighs in , " We will also need , her education and family background verified. " Drago's directive underscores the importance of understanding not just the past situation but also the present circumstances of Karthika's upbringing and associations.

Roma nodded, Drago gave a thumbs-up, and the analyst walked away. The team pursued every lead, making educated guesses based on various possibilities. They began connecting the dots and crafting a narrative that helped them to create a holistic scenario of Operation Morya and hence effectively deal with the security threat at hand.

Chapter 12

Moonlight Musings

The gentle melody of music fills the air, casting a serene ambiance over the beachside restaurant at Novotel, in Juhu, Mumbai. Ovaise reclines in a lounger chair, his gaze drawn to the ethereal beauty of the crescent moon hanging in the evening sky. A voice interrupts his reverie, Geetika, an attractive young woman in her late twenties, accompanied by her slightly chubby associate Neha, draws his attention, "According to a legend, one should not look at the Moon during Ganesha Chaturthi, or the individual will face false accusations and fall from grace." Geetika , states a popular prophecy to Nicolas, as she announces her arrival. Ovaise rises from his seat with a warm smile. He knows he is playing his part as Nicolas Forget - The Documentary Filmmaker and with that, came a natural change in his body language. His French accent was another minor adjustment, as he responded, "One need not worry about this prophecy, if the Vighnaharta is on your side. And by making this documentary, I presume we are in the good books of the Elephant God - Ganpati Bappa. Isn't it!"

Geetika , looks impressed with Nicolas's insight. Nicolas shows his chivalry by pulling out chairs for the two ladies. "The legend of Ganesha Chaturthi and the moon that you just mentioned. The belief only applies on the first day of Ganesha Chaturthi, and we are now well past that. "Nicolas explains. "Well, I am impressed. It seems, the Ganapati Documentary, we are making is in good hands. "Geetika nods in assertion and extends her hand. "Hi, I am Geetika. We have spoken over the phone several times before and I am glad we are finally meeting in person. "Geetika exchanges pleasantries with Nicolas, "And this is Neha Khan, my colleague and junior associate, on the project, from our TV channel. "Geetika adds.

Neha, too, looks impressed with Nicolas's demeanour and knowledge, but she appears to be a little edgier than her usual self. Being upfront had been a part of her working ethic and she didn't hold back her curiosity on this occasion, either. "You look different in the photograph." Neha remarks. Nicolas had trained for moments like this. Without blinking his eyelids, he shifts his gaze towards Neha. "Well, if by that, you mean I look younger than the photograph. Then I will take it as a compliment. Or you can simply call it the French Charme" Accentuating his French tonality, Nicolas tilts his head slightly, in a well-practiced manoeuvre. Neha is swept off her feet, and she blushes. Geetika , laughs, noticing the effect Nicolas has on women, and she also realizes that he had a way with the words, a sign of an excellent storyteller. "Anyway, can we get on with the shoot plan?" Geetika insists. "Well, of course, but let's order first. Wine for you, Nicolas?" Neha suggests and waits for Nicolas to respond. "I don't drink! "Nicolas snaps back, his expression dead serious. Neha and Geetika look at each other in surprise. Nicolas improvises, "Mademoiselle, I am just kidding. How can a French man say no to wine?"

Geetika, Neha and Nicolas break into a laughter and gradually the banter of the documentary shoot takes over.

The wine and the food arrive at their table, and as the three of them, begin discussing the day to day ,shooting schedule, which includes covering various Ganpati Mandal's across the city, a live band starts performing at the beachside restaurant.

RAW Headquarters, Mumbai

26 September, 2023

2000 hrs

Meanwhile, at the RAW headquarters, Munir gets off the phone. His frustration mounts as he struggles to secure assistance from the Ministry of External Affairs for access to the Arabian Embassy. The Ministry of Home Affairs, had already put in a word to the Ministry of External Affairs, but despite his efforts, the bureaucratic deadlock continues; impending their investigation further. "Apparently, there is no official response from the Arabian Embassy, because the envoy is travelling. "Munir declares the situation at hand to Roma and Drago. Drago is quick to respond, "Sir with due respect, *yahaan toh ungli tedhi karke bhi koi fayda naa hai, kyun ki yahaan to ghee hi jama hua hai.* We should shake things up a bit, maybe even heat the container, the ghee will melt and then automatically come out. In simple words, let us put an extraction plan for the key embassy personnel in place and action it immediately "

Munir keeps his frustration in check. It was this impulsive behaviour of Drago, that Munir had problems with, even in the past. Munir declines the proposal politely, and heads back to his office to brainstorm on alternative approaches, to get the ball rolling at the Arabian Embassy. Drago is not surprised. He just looks at Roma, who is undaunted as well by the setback.

To gain fresh perspectives, she delves into the latest data from NETRA and PRISM platforms of the Information Bureau (IB). And just then Drago's phone chimes, it's a mail from Kerala Police. A sense of urgency takes over. Drago quickly rushes back to his desk and opens the detailed report.

It's the first intel on the photograph of 3 ISIS men that an undercover asset from ISIS territory had shared with them. As Drago scrolls through the report, he sees CCTV grabs of the 3 men at the Kochi International Airport two days earlier. The reports state their real names Sadiq, Iqbal and Suleiman with their respective addresses as mentioned in the passports. The detailed report also mentions that the Police had raided the mentioned addresses but there was no one to be found. Drago quickly signals Roma, to go through the latest intel, and gets on the phone to talk to the Kerala Police, POC (Point of contact) N Jagdeeshan.

As Jagdeesan's voice comes alive on the phone, Drago puts the phone on speaker, so that Roma could also hear the conversation. "So far we have found nothing new on these guys, maybe more details will emerge, but there is one thing common between them. They all were reported, "Missing" about 2 years ago" Jagdeesan gives them the key finding of the investigation and adds, "Our initial investigation concurs that the boys had jihadi links and had likely served in the ISIS territory as a militia. "Drago and Roma exchange a glance. They know that the information is unsettling. The presence of these 3 men in the country clearly means that they are sitting on a ticking time bomb, and they need to do better than what they had been up to.

Back at the beachside restaurant in Juhu, Mumbai. The live music band continues to play in the background. Geetika, the Channel Executive Producer, raises a toast, "To a new beginning, and a shoot that, will help us create many more memories." As the trio clink their glasses in anticipation, Neha and Geetika take a sip, while Nicolas covertly empties his wineglass in a flower pot next to him. He is mindful of his beliefs as a devout Muslim. Ovaise focuses his attention on the live band, and he realizes that his secret phone meant only for the mission is vibrating, in his denims pocket, he excuses himself and heads to the washroom.

Nicolas enters the washroom and realizes that there are already a couple of men in there. He washes his face, waits for the two men to leave, and then takes the last WC cubicle in the corner. By turning on the flush, he ensures that anyone entering the washroom won't hear the entire conversation. He takes out his phone, it was Sadiq's call. He dials him back. Sadiq's familiar voice resonates from the other end. "Janab, the sweets for Ganpati festivities had left from Nagor, Rajasthan this morning, and have now crossed over the Gujarat border. The delivery is scheduled to arrive tomorrow, late afternoon, in time for the Ganesha Chaturthi celebrations." Ovaise has a knowing smile on his face. He thanks Sadiq for the update, and as he returns to the beachside restaurant, he transforms back into Nicolas. The music continues to play, and the moon continues to shine, albeit an enveloping shadow, now seems to surround the moon.

BARC Campus, Mumbai

26 September, 2023

2145 hrs

Under the veil of the night, Drago, Munir, and Roma traverse the BARC parking lot, their footsteps echoing against the silence of the surroundings. Roma's voice carries a note of urgency as she voices their collective frustration. "Sir, we are getting stuck. Now we know that 3 ISIS jihadis are on our soil, but we still cannot enforce any counter measures. We desperately need a breakthrough, sir. "Munir nods, "I understand your concern. This only means that the threat is eminent. Kerala Police have circulated intel to all the police stations across the country. And I am hopeful we will have something by tomorrow. "

Drago interjects, "Sir, about the Arabian Embassy incident! I was circumspect at first but with the fresh intel coming from Kochi Airport, I think all these incidents seem to be interconnected. Most importantly, I don't understand why the Arabian Embassy is stalling our investigation."

Munir listens carefully, as Drago continues to link up the incidents and create a compelling narrative, "We have decoded the cipher, we know BARC is under threat, we know the 3 ISIS men are currently in India, and in all probability, they have arrived in Mumbai by now, but we still have nothing on Arabian Embassy. I feel, this embassy intel is the missing link that holds the key to all our answers. "Munir sighs, looks at Roma and Drago, "I agree, but the Arabian Embassy is that padlock to which we don't have the keys yet. "Drago presses on, "Sir, you don't always need a key to enter a house. "Munir snaps at Drago, "Hold it right there, Drago. It is because of this attitude of yours that we have landed in trouble in the past as well. It's a foreign embassy for God's sake!" Munir, Roma and Drago have arrived near Munir's car by now, a brief silence follows, then Roma expresses her concern. "Sir, you are spot on, but Drago also has a point."

Roma emphasizes, " '*Dharmo Rakshati, Raskhitah*' ...Justice when protected protects....This is our motto, but for a judgement to be delivered, justice itself needs to be protected first. " Munir appears intrigued by Roma's interpretation. She adds that

"Nothing can and should stand in the way of protecting our country's sovereignty and for that to happen, no risk is too big and no action too small. "Munir lauds Roma's enthusiasm and throws in a word of caution at the same time , "Look I respect the way you feel for your country but I think your mind is running into an over drive right now." Munir opens the door of his car, trying to subtly put an end to the debate, but Drago had already seen that coming. He takes a step back and responds with a smile, "*Mullah ki daud masjid tak.*" Roma and Munir feel , that it was a direct counter to Munir's argument. Yes, it was exactly meant to do the same, but it was a two pronged tactic, employed by Drago and before Munir could react, Drago adds "I am staying right here at the BARC guest house. "He points at a building in the distance. Drago makes it appear, as if he was just passing on some information, but Munir had got the message loud and clear. Munir had no choice but to consolidate his stand. "About your thoughts on the Arabian Embassy, let's meet with a fresh approach tomorrow morning. Alright!" Munir announces and gets into the car. Roma notices Drago's smart tactical manoeuvre and gets into the car alongside Munir. Tensions simmer beneath the surface, even as Munir's car starts moving.

Drago , starts walking towards the guest house at the BARC campus, getting familiar with his new surroundings, but his mind is already racing, figuring out a way to break in to the Arabian Embassy. The rear side lights of Roma and Munir's car disappear in the distance.

As Roma and Munir drive away in the car, a sense of tension hangs between them. Roma's gaze betrays her curiosity, prompting Munir to lighten the mood. "Drago , is a little odd. On record, he has two houses to his name in Mumbai, but he is never home."

Roma recognizes Munir's attempt to deflect from the underlying tension and plays along. "Indeed," she responds, matching his tone. "His behaviour is rather eccentric. He's quite unpredictable."

She then steers the conversation toward a point of genuine intrigue. "But here's the thing. Yes, Drago is completely off the grid. No Aadhar Card, PAN Card, debit or credit card, not a single digital footprint. He's like a ghost in our digital world, but then how did you manage to track him down?"

Munir nods thoughtfully, turning his gaze toward the passing Ganesha pandals outside the car window. "Remember what I mentioned the other day? 'Follow the dog, and you'll find the man,'" he says cryptically, before turning to face Roma with a dramatic flair. "We've fitted a GPS chip in his dog's collar!" Roma's eyes widen in surprise. It's her turn now to look outside the window and get lost in her thoughts.

Meanwhile, as the night unfolds, a set of nimble feet gracefully alights on the ground, evading the vigilant gaze of BARC's security wall and the ever-watchful eyes of CCTV cameras on the campus. It is Drago, unleashing his unpredictable self. He swiftly flags down a passing black and yellow taxi, an iconic symbol of Mumbai's bustling streets. With determination etched on his face, he instructs the cab driver to head towards the Arabian Embassy at Colaba in South Mumbai. The taxi continues to move through Mumbai streets, already basking in the festive spirit of Ganesha Chaturthi, before making a brief stop at Keerti College Vada Pav, at Dadar. Drago picks up a Chura Pav, his dinner for the night. The taxi continues to pass through Mumbai streets, witnessing the grandeur of the Ganesha Chaturthi celebrations, but mentally Drago is already at the Arabian Embassy.

Chapter 13

The Extraction

BARC Campus, Mumbai

27 September, 2023

0800 hrs

As the sun ascends higher into the sky, its golden rays spill across the grounds of the BARC, casting long shadows and illuminating every corner with a soft, radiant glow. Normally, Mumbai experiences only two seasons, hot and humid summer, which lasts for 8-9 months, and the incessantly wet monsoon , which drenches Mumbai for the remainder of 3-4 months. September brings in the last few weeks of monsoon showers, as Ganpati Bappa comes for his annual visit, but this year the effects of climate change had showed on the Mumbai coast as well. The Sun appears to shine like it's April, the bustling energy of the day begins to awaken, as people emerge from their slumber to embrace the promise of a new day in Mumbai.

Within the confines of the conference room turned command centre at BARC Campus, Drago sits at his makeshift desk. Usually, he is a big fan of freshly brewed filter coffee, but today the coffee cup remains broadly ignored. His attention is captivated by a meticulously arranged set of Jenga blocks that resemble the structure of the Arabian Embassy in his mind. A pair of fresh clothes laid out by his personal attendant are in front of him, but instead of changing into a fresh pair, his mind battles with the 3D layout of the Arabian Embassy.

In the background, we see Munir pacing back and forth, engaging in an animated conversation with the Personal Assistant of the NSA (National Security Advisor). Roma enters the view and signals Munir to join in; he comes in running. Roma slides the Jenga blocks aside. "That was the Arabian Embassy, "Drago exclaims. Roma doesn't get the point and retorts calmly. "It doesn't matter." She places a photograph at the centre of their impromptu layout. "This is Aarif Ahmad, the right-hand man of the Arabian Ambassador. He practically calls the shots. Drago immediately shifts gears and jumps on the moving train of Roma's thoughts. "Family?" Drago inquires. "One wife, two children, but they left the country four days ago," Roma responds matter-of-factly.

"Even though exams are around the corner, they took leave from school," Drago muses. "Four days. Meaning, a day before the satellite signal disappeared, his family had left for Arabia," Munir interjects, with his observation, his voice laden with suspicion.

"The intriguing part is that Aarif himself has been holed up in the embassy for the past four days," Roma adds, exchanging knowing glances with Munir and Drago.

Just then, Munir's phone rings. It's a call back from NSA's office, prompting him to step away and take the call. Engaging in a hushed discussion, Roma and Drago contemplate the probabilities of what lies ahead, while Munir walks back to the opposite corner of the room.

Munir continues briefing the NSA on the phone, "Sir, we have a reason to believe that Mr. Aarif Ahmed from the Arabian Embassy is misusing his diplomatic immunity." The NSA responds over the phone, "You are wasting your time, procuring an official permission to investigate the matter. There are too many red tapes, and you will only end up going around in circles. You'll have to think outside the box." "Are you suggesting a break in?" Munir queries, his expression unreadable. The NSA's response is cryptic: "Yes and no." "Sir, I don't understand," Munir exclaims. NSA has yet another cryptic response, "Take whatever steps you need to take, but *Maine kuch kaha nahin , tumne kuch suna nahin.*- I didn't say any of these things and you didn't hear any of these things." Munir hangs up the phone and heads back to Roma and Drago.

"We need to get inside the Arabian Embassy," Roma insists, her resolve unwavering. Munir remains poker-faced. "Retrieve Aarif," He says. Drago's surprise is palpable, "What do you mean?" *"Maine kuch kaha nahin, tumne kuch suna nahin,"* Munir replies cryptically, leaving his colleagues to decipher the unspoken implications. Roma and Drago exchange a glance., they know they finally have a nod to go ahead. As Munir , walks away, he remembers his interactions with the NSA on the eve of the Uri Surgical Strikes. Incidentally, that day was 27 September, 2016 and today, seven years later, it was 27 September, 2023. It was a similar banter that had ultimately led to India's Surgical Strikes, across the border in POK (Pakistan Occupied Kashmir), on 28 September 2016. It was a retaliation against the Uri Incident in Kashmir.

Sometime later in the day, outside the RAW Command Centre in Mumbai, a van awaits, equipped with an array of sophisticated gadgets manned by tech-savvy operatives. Milind oversees the logistical preparations, his attention soon drawn to the arrival of Drago, clad in traditional Pathani attire replete with a beard and skullcap. Roma joins them, concealing her identity beneath a hijab.

Milind's gaze shifts to Roma's noticeable baby bump, "Madam, are you sure you want to do this?" he asks, his apprehension palpable.

Undeterred, Roma slyly retrieves a small khukhri from her purse, a symbol of her determination and the Gorkha identity, she takes the khukhri dangerously close to Milind. "A Gorkha's daughter should never be told what she can or can't do," She asserts firmly, her conviction unwavering. Drago interjects with a note of practicality. "All that is fine but, this khukhri won't help us get past the security at the embassy"

Roma, acknowledging the limitation, hands the khukhri to Milind with a nod. "I know. I was merely making a point."

Impressed by Roma's resolve, Drago nods approvingly, while Milind relaxes upon taking possession of the khukhri. With determination in their hearts, Roma slams the van door shut, and the vehicle sets in motion, signalling the start of their clandestine mission.

A FEW HOURS EARLIER

Inside the conference room turned command centre at BARC, Drago stands before the assault team, projecting visuals on the screen to aid in his briefing.

Images of Aarif Ahmad flash on the screen, accompanied by a geo-spatial overlay showing the location of the Arabian Embassy. "The satellite signal disappeared at 23:34 hrs on the night of 24 September, at the embassy, with Aarif being the only person present at that hour. It's highly unusual for someone to work so late at the embassy," Drago narrates, his voice echoing through the room.

CCTV footage captures, show a car leaving the embassy premises at 01:15 hrs, further deepening the mystery.

"We made a log of Aarif's car movements, registered under his diplomatic immunity. The data of last 30 days was taken into consideration. Normally, he takes about 20 minutes to travel from the Arabian Embassy to Malabar Hill, his residence. The same was true that night," Drago explains, pausing for emphasis.

"But the next day, his car took a complete detour, traveling from Malabar Hill to Goregaon East, before returning to the embassy," Drago continues, highlighting the visual tracking of the car's route displayed on the huge LED display in front of them.

Drago, presses another switch, revealing the geo-spatial tracking of Aarif's car and actual CCTV footage from various locations, showing Aarif behind the wheel.

"Aarif usually travels with a driver, but interestingly on that night and during the detour to Goregaon, he drove his own car. Furthermore, there was another individual accompanying him," Drago states, zooming in on the blurry visuals of a man occupying the passenger seat.

"The identity of this second individual remains unknown, as does his exact drop-off location, but we will uncover the truth soon," Drago informs, his gaze steady and determined as the team absorbs the gravity of the unfolding mystery." Our agenda for this operation is to pick up Mr. Aarif Ahmad and bring him in."

THE ASSAULT

27 September, 2023

1400 hrs

The sun beats down on the sprawling compound of the Arabian Embassy, casting shadows as the van gets discreetly parked near the back lane. Milind checks the perimeter on his electronic device, ensuring that all is in place for their covert operation.

Inside the embassy, Drago assumes his traditional Pathani attire, a guise intended to facilitate his entry under the pretext of acquiring a visa for Umrah. He appears to be a man in his late 50s and his name, Noor Mohd. Patel. With measured steps, he strides through the entrance, his demeanour calm and composed.

Moments later, Roma follows suit, her form concealed beneath the folds of a hijab, a veil of anonymity that aids her passage through the embassy's security undetected.

Once inside, Drago makes a beeline for the washroom, to gather his bearings and formulate his next move. Meanwhile, Roma approaches the inquiry desk. With practiced nonchalance, she slides her fake passport across the counter for verification, her nerves masked beneath a facade of confidence.

Drago sits on the pot seat in the WC. He removes some tobacco and rolling paper hidden underneath his shoe sole and starts rolling a cigarette. Roma, meanwhile, reaches the second counter where an added level of verification takes place. She realizes the officer suspects something." *Ji naam kya bataya aapne?* What is your name? "The Officer inquires, Roma responds with a beaming smile, "Aashiyana Sultan Mirza" Her ruse is met with further suspicion as the embassy officer flags her passport on his system and decides to retrieve additional information. The officer then makes a call from his desk phone, but the network appears to be constantly busy.

Back in the washroom, Drago , removes the hand dryer cover and pulls out wires, he joins the two live wires to make a spark and light his cigarette. At about the same time, there is a knock on the door, a security guard's inquiry interrupts his solitude. "Uncle, how much time are you going to take? "Drago quips a response in a well-rehearsed Mumbaiya tone, "*Samay to lagega bhai ..budhapa jo hai...woh har cheez slow kar deta hai ....*"

The security guard listens intently, there is no sound for a while so he knocks on the door once again and Drago begins singing, in a low hum "*Lagta hai ab gaana hi gaana padega..... Hoga tumse pyaara kaun, humko to tumse hai, hai kanchi....*"

Back at the counter, No. 2, the officer confirms the details of Aashiyana Sultan Mirza, on his screen. Roma was concerned but sure that Milind and his team would have done a good job in covering all the loose ends of the fake passport. The embassy officer still appears to be dissatisfied. "This is going to take some time. Can you please sit in that line? "The officer points at the bench in the corner. "Once your token number is announced on the screen, you can proceed to the next counter. "He instructs.

Roma, improvises, in the hope, that she will be spared from any further scrutiny, "Is Mr Aarif Ahmad Sahab not available today? My father had asked me to send his regards." " You cannot meet him without prior appointment madam, please take your seat on the bench", the officer replies in a matter-of-fact fashion.

Drago is in the washroom, smoking his cigarette, staring at the smoke detector. He then looks at his watch, when the security guard knocks on the door once again. Drago knows he has to come up with another song in the interim. "*Zindagi ka safar, hai ye kaisa safar, koi samjha nahin koi....*" Drago begins in his uneven tone. "The guard insists. "Uncle, are you downloading shit worth a whole week or what? "Drago presses the flush button, the sound of water flushing down is heard outside. Drago continues to smoke. "My friend, I am almost done."

Roma is seated in a line along with other visa applicants. She is looking at the floor map on the side, to double confirm Aarif Ahmad's cabin location. The next token number is announced, meanwhile a sound is heard in Roma's neatly concealed ear piece. It is Drago. "My list of songs will be over shortly, and the security guard is either under the influence of Diarrohea or he has smelt something funny in me. In either case, you will have to act fast. "Roma realizes she might have to do more than just improvise. "This is unfair," she screams, getting up. "I am observing this for a while now. Everyone else's tokens are steadily moving in line, but I have been at the same juncture for a long time now."

A Junior staff intervenes, trying to pacify Roma, understand her problem, but she creates a scene, nevertheless."I have had enough. I just want to talk to your senior now. When your boss Mr Aarif Ahmad comes to know , how his niece is being treated here, only then you will understand the seriousness of your error. "Junior appears to be a bit intimidated "Sir is in his cabin right now." Roma feels, that the things are finally going her way, she walks in that direction, "Yes take me upstairs, I want to complain about you all, right now. "

The Junior pleads, "Madam, he is in a meeting right now. We will call you when he is done. "

Roma does not stop and goes on to the upper deck, nevertheless. The staff escorts her back immediately, but not before she gets a fair idea of the upper floor and spots , Aarif Ahmad in his cabin. Roma whispers in her earpiece to Drago, "Upper Floor, 3 O'clock right beside the photocopy machine. "

Milind, who has been monitoring the situation from the van parked outside, breathes a sense of relief. He knows it is time for Drago to escalate the matter and take it to the stage 2 of the operation.

Drago swings into action. He takes out the paper napkins from the dispenser in the washroom. He stacks them up in a pile and then uses his cigarette to put it on fire.

The Embassy officer, who had previously suspected Roma, had noticed the ruckus that Roma had created. He instructs the armed guard by his side. "Till any further instructions, your only job will be to keep a watch on her. "The officer implies, pointing towards Roma. On the officer's signal, the armed guard starts moving closer to Roma. Roma is tensed and just then the fire alarm starts blaring. Panic ensues among the embassy staff as the fire alarm blares louder, sending them into a frenzy. The Chief Security Officer who is manning the CCTV console comes running. The sprinklers get activated automatically, chaos ensues. The Embassy Officer is left with no other choice but to initiate the fire drill.

The security guard outside the washroom knocks one last time, in concern. "Uncle shit, all you can, but first save your ass, will you?" The guard rushes to join his team in the fire drill. In complete contrast, Drago appears to be an oasis of calm. He stubs the cigarette under his feet, besides him is the mini bonfire of paper towels, that had triggered the alarm. With a swift moment, he opens the door to direct the smoke from the washroom into the corridor, which adds to the lack of visibility, as well as chaos.

In the corridor, Roma distracts the armed guard, her hairpin transformed into a lethal weapon, she stabs his neck with the hairpin, multiple times. Roma rushes towards the storeroom and starts looking for something frantically. The fire alarm continues to blare and the panicked visitors are being escorted to safety. The Embassy Officer is trying to desperately dial the Fire Service , first by his desk phone and then by his mobile, but to no avail. Just about that time, he notices Roma moving against the tide and searching for something with purpose. He knew something was amiss about the lady from the beginning.

Drago makes it to the top floor. By now, two more armed guards are in the waiting, Aarif Ahmad opens his cabin door at the same time, to move himself and his staff to safety. Drago neutralizes the two guards with his bare hands. Before Aarif can react, Drago grabs his head from behind, pulls out the handkerchief soaked in chloroform, and sedates him.

The Embassy Officer confronts Roma, he takes out his own gun and points it at Roma. He is about to kick her in her stomach. Roma's reflex action clicks in, as she moves sideways to protect her baby. Lucky for her, though, Drago is right behind the officer and he neutralizes the officer with a hit on his neck. All this while, he is still carrying Aarif in his sedated state. Another embassy officer intervenes by this time. Drago counters the officer's punch, using Aarif as a shield. He then lands a powerful kick with his left leg to clear the way ahead. Amidst the chaos of rushing out to safety, and fire alarm still blaring out loudly, two more guards rush towards Drago with their weapons drawn out. Drago is now forced to leave Aarif behind, in an unconscious state. The two officers are now in pursuit of Drago and firing at will. The gunshots add to the chaos, even as Drago leads his pursuers, first through the upper floor, and then through another fire exit. He had memorized the blueprint of the Arabian Embassy, this fire exit was clearly not a part of the blueprint, but he had noticed this exit when he secretly came visiting the embassy on the previous night. On this reconnaissance visit, he had made a mental note of this fire exit as one of the potential exit routes for them. And that is exactly what had come to his aid. Drago takes the exit route, escaping the bullets fired at him, and jams the door with an iron rod, once he is on the other side. The two guards fire more gun shots and finally break down the jammed door. They spread out into the alley, to the left and right, but they only see some random people going about their business. Drago had disappeared, like a ghost.

The guards rush back inside the building, the fire alarm continues to blare, the entire office is in utter disarray, with people queuing up outside the exit. The embassy officials themselves seem to be lost in chaos, with no one to lead them. Roma joins the line, where the security personnel are escorting out the visitors.

In the next few moments, Roma exits the facility. She no longer wears the hijab, instead she has a hijab clad person seated on the wheelchair, which she is pushing out. The hijab has been converted into a burqa to cover the face, and the person on the wheelchair is none other than Aarif Ahmad.

Chapter 14

Kaun Banega Crorepati.......

Farooq, a dignified middle-aged man, stood among the bustling crowd on a busy street. Clad in Thwab—A loose-fitting, long Arabic robe consisting of embroidered pieces that cover most of the body, Farooq exudes an air of quiet elegance as he navigates through the busy marketplace. A warm smile graced his weathered features as he extends a helping hand to his companions- a woman wearing a veil and her two children, their eyes filled with anticipation. The woman, dressed in a flowing abaya and a delicate hijab, appreciates Farooq as he continues assisting them onward. Finally, as they reach the vibrant souk, the children's eyes sparkle with excitement, their mother, Rehana, could not have been happier. She looks at Farooq with gratitude. "Take as much time as you need, stock up on the groceries , and let the children also have some fun, "Farooq says with a smile.

RAW Headquarters, Mumbai

27 September, 2023

1830 hrs

Aarif is beaten black and blue, bruises apparent on his fair skin. They have tied him to a chair, with only a dim light bulb hanging over his head. Milind had been using Aarif as a punching bag, unleashing powerful blows without any restraints. Milind breathes heavily, while Roma watches Aarif and Drago sat in a corner, snacking on some dry chana brought in from the local street vendor.

Aarif's blurred vision hampers his ability to focus on the figures looming over him in the dimly lit interrogation room. Pain pulsed through every inch of his body, each movement sending waves of agony crashing over him. But amidst the haze of pain and fear, one ray of hope echoed in his mind—Diplomatic Immunity.

"You guys are in big trouble. *Mere pass diplomatic immunity hai,*" Aarif croaked, his voice strained with defiance despite the bruises marring his face. Milind's fist collides yet again with Aarif's already battered body, the force of the blow stealing his breath away. "The diplomatic immunity is with your boss, not you. "Milind responds.

Roma watches with a cold detachment, her eyes betraying no emotion as Aarif's torment continued. Aarif knew the game they were playing. He also understood that the stakes were higher than he could have ever imagined. "It's the same thing. You know how it works. It has been more than three hours since I disappeared, following the fake fire incident. It's a matter of time before you get a call from your higher authorities. "Aarif mutters, defiantly.

Just then, the shrill ring of Drago's phone shatters the suffocating tension within the room. Drago knows he has to take the call. He finishes the last bits of dry chana and walks away in the corner to take the call. "We are running out of time, we have a few more minutes at the most, if we get nothing out, we will have to let him go," Munir's voice crackled with urgency from the other side of the phone, the weight of their predicament hanging heavily in the air.

"Yes, sir." Drago's response was curt, his disappointment palpable, but he had not lost hope. Not yet. He types in a message to an unknown number and awaits response. Meanwhile, with a silent nod, he motions for Milind to release Aarif from his restraints.

"Aarif bhai, the orders of your release have already come in, but I have quite a reputation for disregarding the orders. You can check with my colleagues. "Drago speaks sarcastically. Aarif looks at Milind for a reaction, but draws a blank.

Drago now steps intimidatingly closer to Aarif and a dangerous calm settles in the room. "Interestingly, I am also considerate at times, and today happens to be that day. Lucky you!" For the desired effect, Drago claps with his hands and lauds Aarif's chances, then he smiles, revealing his psychotic side.

"So, Aarif, I am going to let you go , after we play a little game, "*Kaun Banega Crorepati*- I love the way you get to choose from so many options "Drago's voice echoes, as he takes a chair opposite Aarif. The overhead light bulb highlights his menacing eyes. Drago removes all the bullets from his gun, except for one. He removes the safety latch and pushes the gun towards Aarif on the table in front of him.

"Option 1 .....this by the way, is my version of the Russian Roulette. You can take your chance and shoot me right now. "Aarif looks at Drago in disbelief, as he continues, "There is only 0.01% chance that you will survive, but while you die, you will at least have the satisfaction that you tried. "Drago implies. Milind and Roma don't know where this is leading but they play along, as they pull out their guns and point it at Aarif.

Aarif's shaky fingers feel the weight of the gun pressing against them. Its cold metal a stark reminder of the odds stacked against him. "Option 2. "Drago resonates, as he removes his watch and puts it on a countdown timer of 3 minutes. "We will simply shoot you at the end of 3 minutes and throw your lifeless body in a drain. The investigators may conclude whatever they want. You shouldn't care really, because you will be already dead by then. "Aarif shoots back a look of concern.

"Option 3–You will give us a minute by minute account about that night, and the man you helped on the eve of Ganesha Chaturthi. "Drago emphasizes. "Your life, your choice. Take a call. Your time starts now. "

Aarif's heart races as he weighs his options. He looks at the gun in front of him and then at the countdown timer placed next to it. Drago had presented him with an impossible choice. Drago's gaze drills into Aarif's psyche, his eyes ablaze with an intensity. He rhythmically taps on the tabletop, adding to the tension, while he mentally rehearses a countermove, in case Aarif picks up the gun. In his heart, though, Drago was counting on the outcome of events that he had set in motion a few hours earlier.

Just then Drago's phone chimes. It's a message from an unknown number. It reads, "We are all set." A sense of anticipation alights Drago's face. He notices Aarif eyeing the gun, still contemplating. "Won't you like to know your 4th option Aarif Bhai? "Drago's eyes pierce through Aarif once again. "By the way, the next one, is less of an option and more of a lifeline,I would say. "Drago's words cut through the suffocating tension, a cruel reminder of the futility of his resistance.

Drago makes a video call. Farooq takes the call on the other side while driving the car. *"Asalam Alaikum Farooq bhai?"* Drago speaks over the phone. *"Walaikum Asalam Dheeraj bhai."* Farooq responds. "Our Bhabhiji and kids are doing fine, I hope? Could you please put them on the phone? " Drago requests.

Aarif's wife Rehana, in an abaya, and the two kids come on screen. They seem to be in a very happy space. Drago hands over the phone to Aarif. With a resigned sigh, Aarif reaches for the phone, his heart heavy with the weight of his choices. A wave of relief washes over him, at the sight of his wife and children, their smiles a fleeting glimpse of the life he longed to return to.

"Why can't I see you on the screen, Aarif? "Rehana sounds a bit concerned. Drago gestures to Aarif. "It seems there is some problem with the network here. I am so happy to see you guys. "Aarif responds and falls in line.

"Thank you for arranging a house help at such a short notice, Aarif. Today, we have got out of the house after four days. The laws on a woman's mobility in Arabia have become more liberal for sure, but you know things don't change overnight. "Rehana's voice was laced with warmth, her words a balm to Aarif's battered soul.

As the call ended, Aarif's gaze lingered on the screen, his heart heavy with the weight of his decisions. In the silence that followed, a sense of resignation settled over him. He knew Drago and his team had cornered him.

Chapter 15

The David Headley Connection....

A camera focuses on a majestic Ganapati Idol inside the vibrant Ganapati Pandal at Khar-Danda in suburban Mumbai. The soft glow of the surrounding lights illuminates its intricate details. The camera gradually trolleys back, revealing the bustling activity of the pandal, and we see Nicolas, the director, and Geetika, the Channel Executive Producer, watching this live feed on a monitor. Behind them, the sparkling décor of the Ganesha Pandal is in its most vibrant display, whereas some political banners of the ruling party are visible on the side. The warm smiles of the politicos on these banners serve as a gentle reminder of the political clout needed to plan such grand celebrations. Additionally, these banners also hint towards the upcoming Legislative Assembly elections in Maharashtra.

Nicolas's expression is the one of quiet satisfaction, as he observes the video footage unfolding before him. His keen eye for detail doesn't go unnoticed as he gives a directive to his team.

"Most Ganesha idols have a left side trunk," Nicolas begins, his voice carrying the weight of authority. "But Ganesha with the right side trunk is rare. Let's make sure that we film one of those."

Geetika's curiosity heightens, and she can't help but question Nicolas's remark.

"Why so?" she asks, her voice filled with intrigue.

Nicolas smiles knowingly, his gaze fixed on the screen displaying the image of the Ganapati Idol, but actually, his eyes are looking at one of the political banners right behind him. The banner features some of the big faces from the ruling party, with the Prime Minister of the country being one of them.

"Worshipping Ganesha with a right side trunk serves the aspect of wish fulfilment," Nicolas explains, "And people widely refer to this form of Ganesha as - Siddhi Vinayak."

Geetika nods, taking in the information, while Neha, their diligent assistant, quickly jots down the point on her notepad. As Geetika watches Nicolas, a sense of admiration fills her. She realizes that behind his calm demeanour lies a deep understanding of cultural nuances and spiritual significance. Little did she know about the months of planning and plotting that had occurred behind the scenes, as Ovaise assumed the identity of Nicolas. Neither was she aware of a chilling terror plot about to be unleashed on her fellow countrymen.

RAW Headquarters, Mumbai

27 September, 2023

2030 hrs

Inside the situation monitoring room, Aarif sat alongside Roma and her team, his gaze fixed on the digital map of Mumbai, displayed on the screen before them. With a sense of urgency, he pointed out the approximate location in Goregaon East, where he had dropped off the mysterious individual.

Roma gestures to her team. Up until now, they were on standby, but now they're actively scanning countless CCTV feeds. Milind, with his analytical prowess, led the charge, scrutinizing the footage for any clues that might lead them to their target. Meanwhile, Drago pushes a cup of piping hot tea towards Aarif, his piercing gaze, still locked onto Aarif, like a hawk, as he pressed for answers.

"What is his name?" Drago's voice cut through the tense silence, his demand for information unfluctuating.

"They don't have names." Aarif responded, his voice tinged with frustration. "I was just told to ensure his safe passage. My job was limited to that."

Roma's team had meanwhile managed to scavenge a CCTV grab of Aarif and Ovaise at the drop-off location, using the indigenously developed IIS- Integrated Intelligence System from the thousands of Giga Bytes of CCTV data at their disposal. Aarif confirms the authenticity of the image with a nod, but the visibility of the image is still unclear because of the distance between the CCTV and the drop off-point. Drago, meanwhile, notices a moment of the hand. He asks Milind to pause and replay the last few seconds. It confirms Drago's suspicion. "What is it? What you are giving him?" Drago muttered, his impatience palpable as he sought answers.

"Sir, it was a parcel which had a film DVD and some rupees," Aarif replies. His words meet with a sharp slap from Drago. "Will you only speak when prompted or what?" Drago's sarcastic remark served as a stark reminder of the seriousness of their situation. Aarif feels the sting from Drago's slap. It hurt him more than the many punches that Milind had delivered. A sense of deafening sensation in his ears gradually settles down.

Roma, undeterred by the tension in the room, instructs her team to upscale the CCTV grab from the drop-off point and run it through their database. With the precision of modern technology and a little help from the machine learning algorithms, the software generated a 3D point cloud and a polygonal mesh of the image. Shortly after, on a side screen, it revealed the probable face of their target.

"He is the one!" Aarif parrots it out this time, without any insistence from Drago- A mix of fear and recognition envelopes him.

Another click of a button reveals 3 people on screen with similar facial features. The picture in the centre has a 97% match to the polygonal mesh. "Ovaise Sheikh," Roma declares the name, her tone somber as she made the connection. "This guy was a trusted ISI operative, but he has been off the radar for almost 3 to 4 years now."

Drago turned to Milind with a sense of urgency, "Formal, informal, I need all the info you can find on Ovaise Sheikh" he commanded, as they delved deeper into the web of intrigue surrounding their elusive target.

Back at the bustling Ganapati Pandal at Khar-Danda in suburban Mumbai, Nicolas and Geetika sat together, having completed their task of reviewing the rushes. With cups of steaming coffee in hand, they took a moment to relax amidst the vibrant energy of the surroundings.

Geetika took a sip of her cappuccino, the warmth of the liquid soothing against her lips as she turned to Nicolas, curiosity glinting in her eyes.

"I have been meaning to ask," she began, her voice outlining her intrigue. "All this knowledge. Is it just for the documentary, or are you just curious by nature?"

Nicolas's eyes twinkled with a hint of amusement. As he considered her question, a small smile emerged at the corners of his lips.

"Actually, it's a bit of both," he confesses, "And I owe this to an old friend of mine. David."

"David?" Geetika echoes. "Yes, David," Nicolas confirms, his voice tinged with nostalgia. "He introduced me to this fascinating land called India. And ever since, I have dreamt of returning here again and again."

Geetika listened intently, captivated by the glimpse into Nicolas's past and the serendipitous chain of events that had led him to their current collaboration. At that moment, amidst the hustle and bustle of the pandal, filled with devotees constantly filtering in and out, she felt a sense of kinship with her colleague, bound together by a shared passion for cinema and storytelling.

RAW Headquarters, Mumbai

27 September, 2023.

2130 hrs

In the Situation Monitoring Room, Aarif is now out of sight. Roma stood before Drago, her expression grave as she pointed to the images of David Headley and Ovaise Sheikh displayed side by side on the screen.

"David Headley, had a significant role in planning the 26/11 attacks. As we all know, David Headley was caught by the American authorities and is currently serving a sentence in their prison. " Roma informs in a matter-of-fact manner, then her voice becomes serious. "When David was in Mumbai for his recce, he was believed to be alone, but the intelligence world is abuzz with a conspiracy theory that he also had an accomplice, who lived in the shadows. His name was Ovaise Sheikh. "Roma explains, her voice tinged with concern

As photos of masked men wielding guns and ISIS flags filled the screen, Roma continued. "New information suggests that Ovaise's absence from ISI of Pakistan is more complex than initially thought. He joined the Caliphate and carried out several ground breaking missions for ISIS. The jihadists eventually gave him a nickname - Quadath-ut-Allah, Fist of God."

Drago's eyes narrows as he absorbs the facts.

"Quadath-ut-Allah - Fist of God. Yes, it is a common term in the Islamic world, used to describe an event, person or an act committed on the behalf of Allah, to avenge the atrocities on the Islamic world. The name says it all," Drago remarks, his voice heavy with foreboding.

Back at the shoot location, the production had wrapped up the shoot for that day, but Geetika was still indulging Nicolas. "If David were here, it would have been even more enjoyable." Nicolas proclaims. Just then, Sameer, one of Ovaise's men who is also working as a production runner for the Documentary shoot, interrupts their conversation. "Sir, someone is here to see you". Having a hand-picked production crew for the shoot had allowed Ovaise to recruit people from their sleeper cells across the county. It gave them a greater control over their operations. Infact, barring his 3 aides, who had joined him from ISIS territory, all the crew members were working professionals from India, but with a jihadi mindset.

Nicolas glances behind the production guy and spots Sahil Patel waiting. Ovaise instantly recognizes Sahil. He was one of the many cogs in the wheel who had continued to play their part in executing the evil machinations of his mind. Ovaise excuses himself, digs into his backpack, pulls out a DVD and walks towards Sahil. Sahil, a modestly dressed office going man, greets him with "*Asalam Walaikum* … "Ovaise cuts him short with a whisper "Not here. "He looks back to ensure Geetika and Neha are away from him. He then speaks in a slightly louder tone with a heavy French accent, to make sure that Geetika hear's this bit. "Sahil, my friend, I am so glad to see you here. The time has finally come. Our hard work of years is finally bearing fruit. "

Ovaise gives Sahil a DVD of the movie "*Hum Dil De Chuke Sanam*" and quietly says, "You'll find the rest of the instructions on this DVD. Remember, completion of this task at your end is crucial to the project, and I know you will not fail me. "Sahil has a non-expressive, serious look on his face. He nods with a sense of determination in his eyes, even as his ID card of AAI – Airports Authority of India dangles from his neck.

RAW Headquarters, Mumbai

27 September, 2023

2300 hrs

Back at the situation room at RAW office, all the officers, including Roma and Munir have left for the day. Milind is still working at his desk, going through the recording of Aarif's interrogation. He has a question in his mind. He looks at Drago, who continues to ponder over the situation board, across his desk.

Drago's eyes remain fixed on the collage of leads on display, but focuses intently on the photo of Ovaise and the deciphered code, Quadath-ut-Allah. Various images of the BARC complex adorn the board, while at the bottom corner is the photo of the three terrorists. The hotline at Milind's desk rings. Milind is quick to respond.

"Drago sir, it's the Kerala Police on line. They seem to have a lead. They want to talk to you. Drago signals Milind to put it on speaker and takes over. "Sir, we have come across an old woman who claims to know one of the three terrorists in the picture. "Drago becomes extra alert. "And what is she saying?" "Sir, she insists on speaking with someone of authority, and in return, she is asking for a favour. "Drago and Milind look at each other. Drago knew witnesses like these could have a personal agenda and that sometimes they provide information that may not even be connected to the case. "Is she reliable?" Drago responds. "She seems to be, sir. She lives in the same area where those three boys used to stay before fleeing to Syria. "Kerala Inspector gives additional input regarding the boys. Drago listens intently before deciding. "Can I speak with her? ..." Drago reconsiders his proposal midway and instead goes with his instincts. "One moment... Have her brought to Mumbai. I'll arrange the pickup for you guys and send you the details." Drago corrects his course, hangs up the phone, and ponders.

"Sir, can I say something... You still seem adrift about something, but I can't fathom why?" Milind interrupts Drago's chain of thoughts.

"When David Headley conducted reconnaissance for 26/11 attacks, BARC was also on his radar." Milind writes David's name beside Ovaise's name on the situation board.

"Sir, we've learned of the proximity between Ovaise and David from our own records. We shouldn't doubt that Ovaise is here to fulfill David Headley's unfinished business," Milind supports his argument.

"David Headley had identified ten other targets for attacks on Mumbai." Drago shoots back. Milind knows Drago is spot on. Drago takes a sip of water. "But that's not the point here. In the world of intelligence, there's a saying that goes, " The truth- *Kumbh Mele mein khoye uss bachhe ki tarah hota hai,*and no matter what happens, *humein uss khoye hue bachhe ko uski maa se milvana hai, wo bhi Kumbh Mela khatam hone se pehle."* Milind reflects on Drago's words. Confusion is apparent on his face. "Imagine you've fallen into a pit, and the only way out is to dig yourself out." Drago tries to explain. "Sir, you are speaking in riddles…" Milind exclaims.

"Indeed, it's a riddle, my friend. We are in the business of intelligence. And the more information we have, the better equipped we are to solve that riddle. Yet, you can never be 100% sure about the intelligence at hand, till it plays out in front of your eyes. "Drago tries to express the workings of his mind.

Milind nods, convinced that there's more to the story than meets the eye. Drago's attention returns to Ovaise and the code, Quadat-Ut-Allah. "Milind, Aarif mentioned about handing over a film DVD to Ovaise, along with the money. I need you to find out more about it." Drago insists.

"Actually, sir, I already have a lead. I wanted to talk to you about the same thing." Milind explains, "The era of the DVD's is gone, but there are still a small set of film aficionados who want to watch foreign films on DVD. Most of these DVDs are pirated, and only a handful of people are involved in this illegal DVD racket." Milind hands out a detailed overview of this report to Drago, and then, in the same instance, he pulls his hand back.

"Sir, can I pursue this lead right away, instead of postponing it till tomorrow, and waiting for others to join in? "Milind requests. "Alright, Milind. Get going. Make it count. We need all the pieces of this puzzle if we're going to crack this." Drago announces.

Milind nods, gratitude and excitement, clear on his face, as he prepares to embark on his solo mission.

Chapter 16

Behind The Bazaar........ (Bhendi Bazaar)

28 September 2023
0800 hrs

At the heart of South Mumbai's Metro Cinema Junction, an iconic Irani Café stands amidst the chaotic rhythm of the maximum city. Its exterior bears the marks of time, with faded signage and weathered paint, yet within its walls lies a treasure trove of history and nostalgia.

The cafe is a sanctuary of old-world charm. The scent of freshly brewed chai and baked cakes filled the air. Vintage furniture filled the cozy space, and tables were decorated with chequered tablecloths. Sepia-toned photographs adorned the walls, and vintage advertisements whispered tales of a bygone era, adding to the café's timeless allure. Amidst the chatter of patrons and the clinking of glasses, conversations flowed freely, weaving a fabric of stories and memories.

The ding-dong of the grandfather clock at 8 AM resonates throughout the cafe. A small, rickety TV beside the clock broadcasts the morning news, featuring the coverage of Ganpati Chaturthi festivities. A man wearing a Parsi cap, navigates through the cafe carrying a plate of baked beans and a Parsi Omelette to a table. In the background, one could hear the faint sounds of morning Ganpati Aarti, from nearby pandals. At the adjacent table, Roma, Munir, and Drago appear to be eagerly awaiting someone's arrival. A cup of tea is each served in front of them, even as they wait for the other breakfast items to arrive.

"What you did with Aarif was risky." Munir breaks silence. "Not knowing about Ovaise Sheikh would've been more risky." Drago reacts non-chalantly. Munir expected more than just a one-line explanation, and this retort particularly ticks him off. He waits for an opportunity to get back.

The Parsi guy places the order on the table. A visibly pregnant Roma takes her Folic Acid and Iron supplements with a glass of water. Drago is more interested in the plate of baked beans. He immediately takes a spoonful. "Hmm.This is the taste of nostalgia. I have been coming here for 15 years but they have neither changed the brand of baked beans nor the taste of their recipe. Can you beat it" Drago announces, relishing on the baked beans.

"*Bean ka brand bhi nahin change kiya bolta hai.* And you figured all this out just by tasting it, right? Oh, wait... I forgot, Dheeraj sir, you're not a man, you're a walking microchip, that comprehends everything in an instant." Munir fires a salvo at Drago. Drago is not much bothered. "Sir, you're over analyzing things unnecessarily. Sometimes, common sense is all that we need." Drago points at the can of baked beans on the top shelf right behind Munir. The shelf has a row of same brand baked bean cans with a placard that reads "Serving Fresh Baked Beans since 2007."

Munir grunts, his past frustrations with Drago also pouring out. "Don't be so sure about yourself. We both know the price we have paid for your overconfidence in the past." Drago places his spoon down, meeting Munir's gaze squarely. Roma feels uneasy with the tension brewing between the two. "*Jaanewale toh chale jaate hai, peeche chod jaate hai kuch sawal*. These unanswered questions, linger like wounds that never heal. Even now, I wonder if I could've done something differently that day." Drago responds, reliving a painful memory from the past.

An awkward silence settles over the table. Roma realizes Munir had hit on a raw nerve of Drago. She wonders , if it was the incident that drove them apart? Understanding that this argument could prolong in an undesired direction, she takes steps to thaw the uneasiness. She begins by clearing her throat, "It seems there is still some time left before Milind arrives, so, let me tell you an interesting story in the interim. And you can guess whether it's fact or fiction? "Munir and Drago, just look at her, without a response, as if they are asking her to just keep out of it, but Roma continues. "Alright, do you know how this market got its name, Bhindi Bazaar? I mean, obviously, no Bhindi/Okra grows here. Right? "Roma realizes neither of the two are interested, but she persists.

"The place we are sitting at is a part of a very old market. In fact, during British rule, even the English had to come here. For every damn thing, from the tobacco, they would smoke, to the meats, lentil and bread they would eat, or medicines they would want to heal, the English had to go behind the bazaar, behind the bazaar...behind the bazaar. Bhendi Bazaar." Finally, Drago and Munir pay attention to this interesting trivia. "So Bhindi Bazaar was an aberration of the word "Behind the Bazaar". Back in the day whatever the white man said sounded cool, so we Indians started copying the aberration too. Slowly but surely, we turned "Behind the Bazaar" into Bhendi Bazaar!"The two of them show enough intrigue, which Roma notices. "So, now that you have heard the story, tell me if this is a fact or fiction? "Roma questions.

"It sounds like a fact", "Munir states nonchalantly. Drago, as usual, has a different perspective: "Whether it's called 'Behind the Bazaar' or 'Bhendi Bazaar,' the crux of the matter is that there was a market here 200 years ago, and there's still a market here today."

Roma jumps in, "Do you have to trivialise anything and everything?" She looks at Drago for a reaction and soon realizes that this could only add fuel to the fire, so she retracts her argument. "Ok, you don't have to answer that." Roma adds, "Listen, we are sitting here waiting for Milind, because we have a job on our hands. "Munir looks at Roma with his brows narrowing. "Let bygones be bygones. You two, get over with your bickering from the past. I don't know about you, but it really makes other people uncomfortable. "Drago looks at Roma. Roma repeats, "Yes I feel uncomfortable, when you go scratching about your pasts. Whatever it is, I don't want to know. All I know is that we have Operation Morya at hand, so let's just focus on that. "

Drago and Munir's expressions suggest that they have got the point. Roma gazes at them in silence, hopeful that this might temporarily ease the tension between the two. In the same breath Roma, notices Milind crossing the Metro Cinema

Junction and walking towards them. Roma also tones down. "Alright, enough with my sermons. Let's get to work now that Milind is here." She looks in the direction of Milind, Munir and Drago, follow her gaze.

Milind has already crossed the road, amidst the crowd and is about to enter the Irani Café, when he suddenly collapses. Milind's sudden collapse sends shockwaves through the bustling street. Drago, Roma, and Munir rush to his aid, and find him bleeding profusely from a gunshot wound in his chest.

Drago instinctively reaches for his gun, while Roma and Munir desperately try to comfort Milind. He struggles to speak but keeps pointing towards the DVD protruding from his pocket. However, everyone focuses their attention on the gunshot wound.

Amidst the chaos, Drago and Munir scan the crowd for any signs of the assailant. There was no sound of a gunshot, indicating the use of a silencer. There are a few hundred people in the street, at that point, but Drago has singled out four potential suspects.

One of them is a pujari engrossed in prayers at the nearby Ganpati Pandal. The second is a skull cap-clad individual, purchasing some maska pav from a makeshift stall right next to the Irani Café. The third is an electrician, and behind them, an office-goer on a bike, who has just screeched to a halt.

Drago is about to chase down the biker, when he does a double take. He turns around and notices the electrician once again. It looks like he doesn't fit in. He wears worn-out shirt and loose-fitting pants, resembling an electrician. Some wires are popping out of his old tattered bag, but his shoes were that of Onitsuka Tiger – the premium Mexican sneakers brand, was a rage amongst the youth. With shoes range starting at an upward of Rs 10,000, it was something he just couldn't have afforded with his low-paying job.

Drago's eyes widens, he takes a step towards him. The young electrician chickens out, he realizes he has been exposed; he drops the wires and fires a shot at Drago in retaliation. Drago wants to fire, but holds back, as he hears Munir's voice, "I need him alive. "

In the heart of Mumbai's bustling streets, the chase unfolds with intensity. The assassin forcefully gets hold of a bike. Drago follows him in pursuit, his mind racing with strategic calculations, his feet sprinting along at a heightened pace. As a Special Forces Operative, his mind had been conditioned to look at the bigger picture, and his brain was already creating a mind map of where the assassin could be headed. The entry that the assassin had taken could only lead to one exit, through a tight lane behind the Mohd. Ali Road. He realized that taking to the rooftops would considerably cut down his time in intercepting the assassin, so wasting no time he takes the plunge breaks open through one of the side alleys and takes it to the rooftop.

Munir, meanwhile, is already on the biker's tail in his car, but the slow-moving traffic on the Mohd. Ali Road ensnares his progress. This, however, works in their favour, as the assassin on the bike slowly seems to get cornered, with one side covered by the non-stop office hour traffic of Mumbai, Drago on the peripheral rooftops and Munir right behind him. In a bid to escape, the assassin abandons the bike on the flyover and jumps into a traffic island right below, covered with some bushes,

Drago's hawk-like eyes, notice the diversion, and takes corrective measures to recalibrate with his target. Munir abandons his car and follows the assassin on foot, while Drago runs in the opposite direction, to enter a bank inside an Old Colonial Building.

The bank staff, in the colonial building had gathered around the Ganpati Idol to do the morning Aarti. The bank manager does a double take as he notices Drago run through his bank office. Ignoring the bewildered stares, Drago ventures into the basement, uncovering a long forgotten secret passage, that was originally built by the Britishers during the World War 2. The long forgotten passage connected the important government buildings in those turbulent times.

Drago, reaches the secret door, but it appears to be jammed. He takes a few steps back and lunges into the door with all his might. The door creaks, Drago, gives it another mighty push, and then another and another. The door finally gives way. Drago , wastes no time and disappears inside the secret passage.

Meanwhile, outside, Munir is right behind the assassin, he crosses the Flora Fountain and heads towards the iconic Kala Ghoda area.

Back at the bank in the old colonial building, the Bank Manager reaches the secret passage in the basement, and looks through the dark alley in amazement. The bank manager is frightened when the bank peon taps his shoulder, holding a thali of Aarti and offering a Modak-shaped ladoo as Prasad. The manager screams, only to realize that it is the bank peon. He is still breathing heavily though, "*Ghelsappa, Prasad, I will eat later, pehle ye bata*. How did this guy know about this secret passage? " The bank manager inquires in his heavy Parsi accent.

The secret alley leads Drago, towards the street , next to the Flora Fountain. As Drago funnels out from the underground stair case, he notices Munir is across the street and just a few meters from the assassin. The assassin is initially headed in the direction of Kala Ghoda, but he suddenly takes a turn and heads towards the Jehangir Art Gallery instead driven by instinct, Drago knows it is time to move in close for the final assault. He cuts right across the street, showing utter disregard to the vehicles passing by. He closes the gap, and lunges forward, but just manages to brush his fingers across the assassin's shoulder. The assassin is off balance. He makes a desperate move to regain the upper hand and shuffles on his right. Drago follows suit. The assassin realizes he will have to make a bolder move, and in that split second instead of moving straight, the assassin again cuts right, almost taking a 90-degree turn ,but instead of managing an escape, he comes right in the path of a fast moving BEST Bus. Drago lunges to push the assassin away from the bus, but he realizes that, the impact is inevitable.

Drago curbs his motion slightly to avoid impacting with the bus,but the assassin has already collided with the bus. Drago gets up back on his feet to notice that the assassin is hit hard. The blood continues to ooze out of his body, making an ever-increasing pool of blood. Besides him lies his half open side bag, which is full of Hindi film DVD's, Drago is too overwhelmed with the adrenaline rush that he does not register the bag yet. He is no medical expert, but he is still analysing the chances of the assassin's survival. Munir reaches the spot in the next few seconds. He looks at Drago, who is still in his element.

The scene across the Jehangir Art Gallery is fraught with tension as medical staff rushes to attend to the badly injured assassin. Munir takes charge, supervising the accident scene with a keen eye, while the area is cordoned off by police, as they begin a meticulous documentation of the accident scene.

"Please ensure all of this man's belongings are taken into custody and sent to the RAW office." Munir instructs the Sub -Inspector of Police at the accident site.

Munir's phone buzzes, signalling a call from the DGP's office. He steps aside to answer the call, leaving Drago to keep a watchful eye on the unconscious assassin. Drago approaches the attending doctor, seeking some assurances. "Will he survive this?, Drago inquires. " We can't say for certain. It appears there may be some serious internal injuries." The young Doctor manning the emergency vehicle responds. In his head, though, Drago has made his calculations. By the time this guy would recover, that is, if he recovers; the terror plan would have been executed, and hence his survival held little significance, for Operation Morya at least.

As the ambulance door closes and the vehicle speeds away, Drago mutters in frustration. "Another dead end."

Munir meanwhile, concludes his call and joins Drago, to relay the information. "The DGP has summoned me." I think they're considering sanctioning the extra force we had requested. I will meet the DGP right away and see you at the RAW office."

Drago nods. Munir, walks away with a sense of urgency. Drago's mind digresses away for the first time. He wonders , if Milind had survived the gunshot?

Chapter 17

Sweets From Nagor....

Dadar Flower Market, Mumbai

28 September, 2023

1100 hrs

During the auspicious occasion of Ganesha Chaturthi, the Dadar Flower Market transforms into a kaleidoscope of devotion and festivity. Devotees flock to the market in huge numbers, seeking vibrant blooms to adorn the idols of Lord Ganesha. It super charges the surroundings with excitement and anticipation.

The market's busy lanes become even more crowded as vendors create elaborate displays. Strings of bright orange marigold flowers are draped across makeshift stalls, fragrant jasmine flower buds are carefully woven into intricate floral arrangements, while lotus blooms stand as a symbol of purity and auspiciousness. Amidst the floral parade, the market resonates with the sounds of traditional music and chants, adding to the festive ambiance. Additionally, the vendors peddle an array of decorative items, ranging from colorful torans (door hangings) to intricately crafted garlands adorned with beads and sequins, each designed to enhance the grandeur of the Ganesha Idols.

The Dadar Flower Market during Ganesha Chaturthi is not just a place to buy flowers; it is a vibrant hub of culture, tradition, and shared reverence for Lord Ganesha. This is exactly what Nicolas and his team had set out to capture when they arrived at the Dadar Flower Market in the wee hours of the morning.

In the makeshift shooting tent at Dadar Market, Geetika expressed her displeasure with the rushes she had seen on the small monitor. She thought the shots called for improvisation and wanted to communicate her suggestions to Nicolas, but he was not in sight. Geetika tries to contact Nicolas on the walkie talkie, but there's no response. Noticing Nicolas's walkie-talkie on a nearby table, she realizes he had not taken the walkie with him.

Geetika walks out of the tent, the spot boy is quick to attend her. "Where is Nicolas?" she demands. "I have no idea," the spot boy replies, scanning the market in every direction. He states he left after receiving a phone call. "They were talking about some sweets or something," he adds. "Mithai ?" Geetika grunts in disapproval.

The spot boy's gaze continues to roam around the market, and suddenly he spots Nicolas at the distant end of the market. He singles out Nicolas amidst the crowd, for Geetika, and she marches towards him. Seeing him take a turn at the far end, Geetika quickens her pace.

Nicolas, meanwhile, follows the driver, who is leading him inside the back of a trailer truck filled with mithai boxes.

In order to make room at the backside, some boxes had to be removed. The driver then leads him to a huge rectangular box enclosed in a wooden frame and leaves by himself. Nicolas makes sure he's alone, then takes off the wooden cover and the protective layer beneath. A smile beams through his face. He is looking at a menacing looking cylindrical packaging. It is not big enough to be called a missile, but it looks like a cutting edge, state-of-the art weapon system, fitted with a launch pad, and different sensors. "Quadath-Ut-Allah," Nicolas mumbles, as he runs his fingers over the deadly weapon.

Geetika walks through the flower market. She passes the turn that Nicolas had taken and then stops after a few meters. It dawns on her, she has missed the turn. She walks back a few steps, manoeuvring through the crowded lane and then takes the narrow alley leading to the godown.

As Geetika walks deeper and deeper into the alley, the chaos of the flower market appears to be left behind. She walks into the godown. The place looks shady and Nicolas is nowhere to be seen, but she spots the half open trailer truck filled with mithai boxes. She wonders if Nicolas is there and ventures inside.

Unaware of all this, Nicolas is paying off the driver, in the front side of the truck. The driver assures him that the smaller parcels of mithai will directly reach them at the depot in Goregaon East, later that night in a separate truck. They had separated the cargo for security reasons; he explains.

Nicolas climbs back into the truck, to notice Geetika. She appears to be hovering over the wooden box. She bends lower to have a closer look. Nicolas realizes anything could happen at this moment, but he also realizes that Geetika had still not served her purpose. He decides, he would only kill her as a last resort.

He calmly brings out his gun from behind and removes the safety latch. Just then Geetika's phone vibrates, it is an incoming call from Neha. Just as Geetika turns around to leave, she is startled to find Nicolas standing right in front of her. Nicolas hides the gun behind his back, just in time. "Hey Geetika," he mumbles, trying to improvise. "Where the hell have you been?" Geetika, asks, retaining normalcy after the initial shock. Nicolas desperately tries to come up with an answer. "Well, aaa.aa. ....I learnt about these guys. "He fumbles, but continues to weave a story, nevertheless. "The local Ganesha mandals call for this specially made mithai all the way from Nagaur, in Rajasthan, which is more than a 1000 kms from here. I thought it could be an interesting piece for our documentary."

Geetika does not look convinced. The disappointment of the B roll shots she had seen earlier, continues to play on her mind. Geetika stares intensely at Nicolas.

Nicolas has read Geetika's mind. He knows the dice could still roll either way; he continues to hold his gun, with the finger on the trigger, ready to fire at a fraction's notice. Tension builds up. Geetika removes something from her pocket. Nicolas is about to draw the gun, when Nicolas realizes it is his walkie talkie. Geetika hands over the walkie back to him, " We need to redo a couple of shots and next time, don't disappear on me without informing." Nicolas watches Geetika get out of the truck and walk away, Nicolas, breathes a sigh of relief .He realizes, he needs to be more careful.

Milind's House

28 September, 2023

1630 hrs

The somber atmosphere of Milind's home is palpable, the grief of Milind's parents evident in their pained expressions. The body had been taken in for postmortem, but the near and dear ones had gathered to express their support to Milind's family. Roma and Drago stand side by side in a corner, their expressions heavy with sorrow, a silent understanding passing between them. The faint traces of Milind's blood still clinging to Roma and Dheeraj's clothes serve as a poignant reminder of the fragility of life. "He was such a bright chap, always full of enthusiasm. It's still hard to believe we've lost him." Roma's voice trembles as she speaks.

Drago is abhorrent, as he remembers Milind in his arms, after getting shot by the unknown assassin, earlier that morning. Drago recollects how he was true to his duty. Even in his dying moments, he was trying to say something, but words failed him. The bullet had pierced through his back and punctured his lungs, with blood oozing continuously. Roma had immediately called for an ambulance, and rushed Milind to the Bombay Hospital, but he had passed, even before they reached the hospital. Drago felt terrible, that in Milind's dying moments, Drago had to choose between his colleague and the call of duty. Drago described such moments as a soldier's curse, and unfortunately, he had experienced it more than once.

Drago wanted to cry, but his tears failed him. A teary-eyed Roma notices the internal struggle of Dheeraj. "You want to cry, but the tears won't come. They describe people like you as - tortured perfectionists. They train you to control your emotions, I understand that, but sometimes it's okay to let it out." Roma puts her hand on Dheeraj's shoulders, pacifying him. It was in vulnerable moments like these, when Drago became Dheeraj. His mind drifting back to the time,when he was a 10-year-old boy.

Srinagar, Kashmir

1989

The year was 1989, and his father was stationed in what was considered as the "Heaven on Earth" at that time - Kashmir. However, with Pakistan rolling out its proxy war in the valley, there was a significant rise in militant insurgency, and the situation had deteriorated in a matter of weeks. One fine day, Dheeraj's father dressed in his army uniform was dropping him off at the school, when a couple of militants came on a motorbike. They opened fire at Dheeraj's father and emptied a full magazine of bullets with their assault rifle. Dheeraj cried helplessly as he watched his father meet his tragic end.

At the last rites of his martyred father, his father was brought in a coffin, with the tricolour flag draped over it. His mother cried hysterically, but he battled his tears, even pacified his mother. He swore revenge, and took a vow that day, that he will never ever shed a drop of tear on a soldier's martyrdom. Unknowingly so, the child in him had become a man, and he took the first step in transforming from Dheeraj to Drago.

Milind's House

28 September, 2023

1700 hrs

Back at Milind's house, the buzzing of his mobile phone jolted Drago out of his reverie. It was Munir. "Where are you, sir? You should have been here, at Milind's place. I've been trying to reach you." Drago whispers. Munir understands the delicate situation, but he also knows there is no time to waste, he cuts to the chase. "Drago, we're not getting any extra forces, as we thought. And there's more news. I have been ordered to stay with the SPG- Special Protection Group for tomorrow's election rally by the Prime Minister at BKC." Drago questions him, still trying to grasp this new development, when Munir informs him, "You are now the First in Command for Operation Morya."

Confusion clouds Dheeraj's mind as he passes the phone to Roma. Roma hears Munir's full account. Dheeraj and Roma exchange a glance, their thoughts racing amidst the chaos, even as grief and uncertainty continues to envelope them. Meanwhile, the sound of azan overlaps.

Light Equipment Godown

28 September, 2023

2240 hrs

The prayers of Esha Salah, the night time namaz, is audible in the background. In the dimly lit confines of the light equipment godown, a sombre congregation of Ovaises's men knelt in unified devotion. Their prayers formed a silent crescendo amidst the backdrop of their makeshift command centre.

On the fringes of their sanctuary, the real Documentary Film Maker- Nicolas Forget, finds himself in dire straits. A wooden box with assault rifles and lots of ammunition lies in the open at a distance of about 10 ft from him. He is bound by hand and foot; he wants to scream, somehow raise an alarm to alert others, but with his bullet wound slowly becoming septic, and the constant shots of morphine infused into him, he is just an unwilling spectator to the night's proceedings. By his other side is an elaborately crafted Ganesha Idol in its finished form. Nearby, a secondhand two-wheeler stood in readiness, its presence overshadowed by the imposing silhouette of a red tanker, its chassis under a fresh coat of paint. As the final words of their prayers hung in the air, Ovaise rose, folding his prayer carpet with deliberate care. He turned to address his men, his voice laced with a commanding presence that demanded undivided attention.

"The time to seize our mission is upon us. Success lies just around the corner, and it is at this juncture that I wish to express my gratitude to all of you. Each of you knows the role you must play," he declared, his gaze sweeping across the faces of his comrades. In a unified response, his men affirmed their readiness, their voices merging into a single vow of allegiance.

"Mashallah, then our next meeting shall be over our enemy's dead bodies. " Ovaise continued, his proclamation hanging in the air, like a solemn oath.

Riaz, the techie, distinguishable by his geeky demeanour, approached the real Nicolas with an offering of food, a small gesture of humanity amidst the prevailing tension. Meanwhile, the others retreated to their makeshift beds, seeking a few hours of rest before the dawn of their fateful day.

Sadiq, tasked with a critical role, attended to the two-wheeler with meticulous care. As he started the ignition, the vehicle's engine sprung to life with a reassuring rhythm. Ovaise approached him, placing a hand on Sadiq's shoulder in a gesture of camaraderie and trust.

"Is your bride under control?" Ovaise inquired, his voice laced with an unspoken urgency.

"She is well aware of the consequences if she chooses not to comply. The safety of her child ensures her cooperation. Everything is under control," Sadiq replies, his tone resolute.

"Excellent. There must be no room for error tomorrow," Ovaise's words echo the weight of their impending task.

Sadiq looks back reassuringly. Ovaise then hands over a bunch of badges to Sadiq. "These are your crew tags for tomorrow. Geetika and the Television Office already know that there will be extra crew tomorrow for the different camera rigs, and other production pieces."Sadiq nods.

Ovaise walks over to the Uri Strikes exhibit, conducting last-minute checks. "Make sure you transport the Ganpati Idol and this decorative exhibit representing the Uri Strikes to the TV office in time." "Consider it done." Sadiq responds as he places the crew badges safely in his bag.

With a final nod, Sadiq, takes his leave, manoeuvring the two-wheeler, through the godown's complicated corridors and out into the quiet of the night. Ovaise had to still make a series of calls , and coordinate with the other sleeper cell recruits, placed at a different location in South Mumbai. He knew even they would have to play a role to ensure that their ultimate plan was successful.

The scene fades away, leaving behind a wave of anxiety that spoke volumes of the impending dawn and an uncertain destiny that awaited them all.

Chapter 18

The Prelude

29 September, 2023

1000 hrs

Private jets and luxury aircraft dotted the Juhu Airport, creating an air of opulence. A unique aviation hub reserved only for VVIP flights, this airport in Mumbai caters to the society's elite and the high-ranking government officials.

Sunlight reflecting off the glass facades of the terminal building gave it a polished and sophisticated look. Inside, plush lounges and VIP suites provided a sanctuary for discerning travelers, with attentive staff catering to their needs.

Armed guards and surveillance cameras discreetly maintained a sense of vigil around the airport, ensuring the safety of the premises, whereas the meticulously maintained and illuminated runway was ever ready to welcome dignitaries and VIPs from all over the world.

Today, was one such day where a Boeing 737 - Business Liner gracefully touched down on the runway, bearing the call sign AIR INDIA ONE, a Special Extra Section Flight operated by the Indian Air Force for the President of India, Vice-President of India or Prime Minister of India.

The engines of the Boeing Aircraft slow down to a softer hum. The sunlight glints off its sleek exterior, as it taxis towards the docking area. With a gentle hiss, the plane comes to a stop, and the door swings open, revealing the figure of the Prime Minister.

Stepping out onto the tarmac, a flurry of activity greets him. A convoy of sleek cars, flanked by stern-faced Commandos of the SPG-Special Protection Group, awaits him. Among the special dignitaries present to receive the PM stands Munir, a picture of composed anticipation.

Inside the bustling AIR TRAFFIC CONTROL TOWER, Sahil Patel sits before a bank of monitors, his fingers dancing across the keyboard as he feeds the data of the incoming and outgoing flights. The arrival of the Prime Minister's Aircraft is duly noted by him, in the official log. He looks around and ensures that his colleagues are busy at their desk, then he walks away to take a washroom break. A flicker of recognition crosses his face, as he recalls his previous meeting with Ovaise Sheikh-A memory tinged with intrigue, and he is determined to pull off his part of the job. He reaches the washroom, takes the last cubicle, and then instead of sitting on the pot, he pulls down the seat cover and climbs on top of it. From the false ceiling, he retrieves another mobile phone that he had smuggled inside the airport a few days earlier. He powers up the old, no-frills feature phone. Quickly, he types out a message, sets the phone to silent mode, and slips it into his pocket. His hands are already shaking in anticipation. He is breathing heavily, so he closes his eyes and tries to calm himself down.

Bandra West, Mumbai

29 September, 2023

1015 hrs

Surrounded by the vibrant chaos of the Ganpati Pandals, Nicolas stands in the midst of a bustling crowd, his phone alerting him with a message. A smile tugs at the corners of his lips as he reads the message. Meanwhile, the crew scrambles around him, swiftly assembling their equipment in preparation for moving to the next location. "Geetika?" Nicolas calls out, his voice cutting through the ruckus.

Geetika, engrossed in conversation with the remainder of her crew, swiftly breaks away, her steps purposeful as she approaches Nicolas.

"Yes, Nicolas?" Geetika inquires, her demeanour attentive.

"I was reviewing the footage from the day before yesterday," Nicolas begins, his tone measured. "I'm not happy with the shots we have taken at the GSB Mandal in Chembur near BARC. It has similar issues like the one you pointed out yesterday. I think we need to reshoot the bits. "

A hint of concern flashes across Geetika's features. "Oh... alright, but going to Chembur and back. Won't you get late for the next location? We will need time to prep up as well, "Geetika responded, her mind already racing to accommodate the unexpected change in plans.

"Don't worry," Nicolas reassures her, a determined glint is visible in his eyes. "It won't take long. I'll take a skeletal crew with me. The rest of you can head back to the office and start setting up. We should be done and back at the location within an hour or two. Besides, the extra hands that I had asked for have already reached the location, and started prepping up for the shoot scheduled for later today."

Geetika nods, her expression purposeful. "Okay, sounds like a plan. But keep in mind, today is Ganesh-Gauri Visarjan. of Ganesh Chaturthi. It is one of the biggest days for Ganesh Visarjan. Things are going to get busy real soon. I want you to capture every bit of the Visarjan, as devotees get ready to immerse Ganpati Bappa idols, in the sea. Let's try to stay on schedule. Alright!"

Owing to their shared understanding, Nicolas acknowledges her concern with a thumbs up, it was a silent promise to remain focused amidst the impending chaos. Ironically, though, they both had very different end goals in mind.

Bandra Kurla Complex, Mumbai

29 September, 2023

1130 hrs

In another part of the city, not too far away from where Nicolas is; the convoy of the Prime Minister snakes through the bustling streets of Mumbai. the anticipation in the air is palpable. Crowds line the roads, their excitement mounting as they catch glimpses of the passing entourage. Finally, the convoy arrives at the BKC Grounds, the site of a massive political rally.

Thousands of people had assembled, creating an electrifying atmosphere with their cheers and chants." PM, PM, PM….." Munir emerges from one of the cars in the PM's entourage, his demeanour focused, as he takes charge of securing the perimeter. However, his efforts are challenged by the uproarious noise emanating from the sea of eager supporters.

Unfazed, Munir continues forward, purposefully maneuvering through the crowds. As he surveys the scene, a sense of responsibility weighs heavily on his shoulders. Witnessing the fervour of the rally, and given the popularity of the PM, he knows that maintaining law and order and ensuring the safety of all present will be a delicate task, but the SPG had it all worked out, and they practically did this day in, day out. Then Munir's mind momentarily drifts towards Milind. He could not even meet his family in their hour of grief. He was even more concerned that the burden of Operation Morya had passed on to Drago, Roma, and the team. The task of averting a potential nuclear blast was nothing short of a nightmare. With no more leads on the table, he was feeling frustrated, and somewhere he had sensed that the final countdown for Operation Morya had begun.

Chapter 19
The Chaos

Chembur Police Station, Mumbai

29 September, 2023

1200 hrs

Amidst the muted buzz of activity, a scene of cultural discord unfolds within the four walls of the Chembur Police Station in Mumbai. The old lady from Kozikode, who offered intel on Sadiq, is sitting at the table with an accompanying policeman, but they both seem out of place. They are talking to the Head Constable of Chembur Police Station. The air is thick with tension and laced with misunderstanding.

The elderly lady Mrs. Nair from Kozikode shakes her head in denial, her features etched with a plea as she addresses the officers gathered before her in broken English. "I've already told you," she implores, her voice trembling with frustration. "I'll only speak to your superior...please."

Across from her, the constable exchanges a knowing glance with his senior, a silent acknowledgment passing between them as they navigate the delicate situation.

"This Madrasi is quite stubborn, sir," the constable remarks, his tone tinged with resignation. "Perhaps if we speak to her firmly, she'll open up."

The Policeman from Kerala interjects, his voice laced with irritation, as he seeks to correct a misrepresentation. "She's not Madrasi," he protests, "She's a Malayalee."

"Yes, yes, but Malayalee and Madrasi are the same thing... naa," the constable concedes with awkwardness in his words. The Kerala Policeman, appears to be angrier than before.

Chembur, Mumbai

29 September, 2023

1215 hrs

The pulsating beat of the city's Ganesh Chaturthi festivities fills the air as Ovaise's car effortlessly weaves through the crowded streets of Chembur. It appears that some of the pandals have already begun preparing for the Ganesh-Gauri Visarjan. The car passes a signboard that reads BARC -1 Km, while GSB -Seva Mandal is indicated towards the right. Ovaise's gaze shifts to the right, drawn to the sign indicating GSB Seva Mandal. With a decisive nod, the car veers right, steering towards their destination.

Outside the Ganpati Pandal of GSB Seva Mandal, the car stops, and you can almost feel the vibrant energy of the surroundings. Ovaise steps outside and glances at his watch, realizing it's 12:20 PM. With purposeful strides, he directs his crew, his gestures animated, as he choreographs the camera movement for the scene. "Take B-roll shots from different angles," he instructs, his voice cutting through the chaos. Three of his crew members just nod, knowing well that all this was just to put up a show. Positioning himself under a nearby tree, Ovaise surveys the surroundings with a critical eye. He once again looks at the watch and then waits.

Chembur Police Station, Mumbai

29 September, 2023

1225 hrs

Drago and Roma stride into the room of the Chembur Police Station, their expressions a mix of determination and empathy. Their gaze falls upon the old lady, who has been anxiously waiting along with the Kerala Policeman. Before anyone can react, she rushes towards Drago, desperation etched on every line of her face. "Please, sir, find my daughter. Find my daughter, " she pleads. Drago and Roma exchange a glance. They were told that the lady in the waiting knew something about the terror suspects from ISIS.

With practiced gentleness, Drago and Roma approach her, their expressions softening as they guide her to a nearby chair, offering a semblance of comfort amidst the turmoil of her emotions. Roma signals to bring in some tea for Mrs. Nair, and the Kerala Policeman. At Drago's signal, Roma places a photo of three suspected terrorists in front of her. "We will do everything possible to help you. But first, you need to tell us what information you have about them."

With tears in her eyes, the old lady nods firmly, determined to share her story. "I promise," she says, her voice barely above a whisper. "And you'll find my daughter, right?"

Drago reaches out and grasps her trembling hand, silently promising her to bring closure to her anguished search. With a trembling finger, the old lady points to one face in the photo, her voice trembles as she recounts her tale of loss and longing.

"He is my *Marumaakan,* my son-in-law," she starts, her voice wavering a bit. "My daughter was already married, with a three-year-old child. Then one day, tragedy struck, and her husband was taken from us in a road accident. "

As she drinks water, her past wounds resurface. "This Sadiq fellow appeared in her life from out of the blue. He wasn't a good man, I knew, but before I could do something, my daughter and Sadiq eloped in the dead of the night."

She left behind a letter explicitly stating not to contact her. Mrs Nair adds, "It's been close to one and a half years... I've been searching for my daughter. I haven't found her, but then I saw this photo of Sadiq on TV."

BARC, Chembur, Mumbai.

29 September, 2023

1230 hrs

A car glides to a halt at the main gate of BARC, its engine purring softly as a woman steps out and heads to the security cabin. Security personnel swarm around her, meticulously checking her with a metal detector before scrutinizing her ID. Satisfied that she is an employee, her bag is put through a scanner and they allow her to pass through the gates. Moments later, another figure emerges, this time on a two-wheeler. Dressed in a traditional salwaar kameez, the woman exudes a quiet demeanour. The security scans the ID. It is a match; the screen reads - Karthika Nair, and along with that a small alert pops onto the screen. The security personnel exchange a knowing glance and flag it on the system.

The security puts her bag through the scanner and she opens her two-wheeler dickey for manual inspection. She appears to be lost in thought. Torn between her dual identities of Karthika Nair and Fatima, motherhood was the only aspect of her persona that was keeping her being intact. She was thinking about her son, Rizwan. Sadiq had made the two of them talk over a video call that morning. The security personnel meanwhile, had scanned her bag and checked her vehicle two times over. He instructs Karthika to put her vehicle in the parking area and head to the admin building.

Chembur Police Station.

29 September, 2023

1235 hrs

Back at the police station, Roma's phone starts buzzing, but she does not want to be distracted by the ongoing conversation with Mrs. Nair, either. She is unable to decide, but when the phone rings for a second time, she feels compelled to move aside and take the call.

Meanwhile, Mrs. Nair digs into her purse, with trembling hands, she retrieves the marriage photograph of her daughter and Sadiq, that her daughter had left behind with the letter. The old lady implies, "This is my daughter, Karthika."

At about the same time, Roma turns around to update Drago. "Karthika has just entered BARC." Drago looks at the photo in front of him. He draws Roma's attention towards the photo and connects the dots. "Isn't she the one on Leave Without Pay for the past three months?" Roma has a closer look at the photograph and nods. With a knowing glance, Roma and Drago exchange an unspoken understanding, their senses heightened. Drago instructs the Inspector in -charge to take good care of the old lady and without a moment's hesitation, both him and Roma rush out of the Chembur Police Station.

In the next few moments, both Roma and Drago are in the Interceptor Car that they had been driving ever since Operation Morya had become operational. The duo head back to BARC campus as fast as they can.

Back at the BARC Campus, Karthika parks her two-wheeler in the designated parking area and starts moving towards the admin building. Karthika was clueless about the exact inclinations of her husband Sadiq. All he had asked was to rejoin the office from today. Sadiq had helped her make up a story to explain her prolonged absence. Karthika was just rehearsing the same as she approached the administration building of the BARC. All that she needed to do was to ensure that she was in the office building before 12:40 PM. Sadiq had heavily emphasized on the timing. Karthika, aka Fatima, looks at the watch. It is 12: 39 PM, the security clearance had taken more time than expected, and with just one minute left to 12: 40 PM, she quickens her pace.

GSB Seva Mandal, Chembur

29 September, 2023

1239 hrs

The crew, at BARC, take a Dolly Zoom Shot of the Ganesha Idol at the GSB Seva Mandal, to recreate the iconic vertigo effect shot for their documentary. However, Ovaise is least interested in that and instead concentrates his focus on his watch. As the watch displays 12:40 PM, he takes out another mobile and dials a number.

The driver of Roma and Drago's car is doing the best he can, but thc traffic is heavy and their car gets stuck a few hundred meters before the BARC campus. Drago, calls CISF Chief, at BARC who was already aware of Karthika's presence at the campus. The Chief was already on his way to take Karthika in custody. Drago emphasizes the need to detain Karthika and keep her under surveillance. He predicts it is about time for shit to hit the roof.

GSB Seva Mandal, Chembur

29 September, 2023

1240 hrs

Ovaises's phone connects with another phone, the phone rings and what follows is a momentary silence.

BARC, Chembur, Mumbai

29 September, 2023

1240 hrs

Karthika is a few steps away from the administrative building. Moments of silence, overlaps the sound of a mobile phone connecting with other mobile phone. Karthika, could hear the faint sound of a mobile ringing. Then, a deafening blast rips through the air, sending shockwaves reverberating through the surroundings. Karthika's two-wheeler is torn apart in a fraction of a second and reduced to nothing but twisted metal fragments scattered across the pavement. Karthika is thrown into the air by the sheer force of the IED- Improvised Explosive Device.

Traffic Signal, Near BARC

29 September, 2023.
1240 hrs

Drago and Roma freeze, hearing the distant sound of the explosion. Drago signals Roma to call in for the backup and swiftly exits the car. He sprints purposefully, his gaze fixed on the distant BARC complex, still a couple of hundred meters away.

Chaos reigns within the BARC Campus as CISF personnel scramble into action. Their training kicks in as they rush to contain the unfolding crisis. Armed with fire extinguishers, some of them swiftly move towards the epicentre of the disturbance, their faces etched with grim determination.

Within moments, the wail of a fire brigade siren fills the air as it races towards the BARC gate. The two CISF men at the gate wonder for a moment that the fire brigade's response was much swifter than expected. They are relieved nevertheless, and they direct the brigade towards the blast site.

Meanwhile, at the blast site, two CISF men stand vigilant, their eyes scanning the horizon as they await the arrival of reinforcements. Suddenly, the air is filled with the sound of approaching sirens, and within moments, the fire brigade screeches to a halt at the scene.

Three firefighters disembark from the vehicle, their movements quick and precise as they rush towards the source of the flames. With practiced efficiency, they aim their hoses at the blazing wreckage of what used to be Karthika's two-wheeler, with an intent on quelling the inferno.

However, their efforts are in vain, the flames roar even more defiantly, as soon as the discharged liquid comes in contact with the burning vehicle. An invisible force seems to power the burning wreckage. Panic sets in as the realization dawns, that the water tanker was actually filled with petrol—and the firemen are not who they appear to be. With chilling precision, they draw concealed weapons and open fire on the unsuspecting CISF personnel, catching them off guard. The firemen are none other than Oviase's men, from the light equipment godown, and the fire brigade is the vehicle they were repainting at the godown.

Amidst the chaos, Drago's figure emerges on the scene, his presence a beacon of hope amidst the turmoil. With a nod of acknowledgement to the CISF men, he sets about coordinating a counter response to the escalating crisis.

The three terrorists, their identities concealed behind masks of deceit, scatter like shadows, each disappearing into the complex corridors of the BARC Campus. Their weapons drawn, they take up strategic positions, firing at will. The remaining CISF men on the campus launch a counterattack. The petrol tanker, meanwhile, starts moving away.

With a sense of urgency, Drago joins the ensuing gun battle between, CISF men and the terrorists. Drago is under heavy fire. He manages to find cover behind some trees and starts firing back with a vengeance. Soon enough, his bullet finds the mark and kills a terrorist. Drago swiftly moves in the shadows to join the rest of the CISF team, who are exchanging fire with two other gunmen. At about that time, Drago notices the fire brigade filled with Petrol edging perilously closer to the nuclear dump site.

The realization hits Drago that the petrol-laden tanker is a ticking time bomb, capable of causing disastrous consequences. He takes control of a nearby CISF Jeep, his gaze fixed on the looming threat before him. With time running out, he skillfully navigates through the chaos, determined to reach the petrol-filled Fire Brigade Tanker.

The driver of the Fire Brigade was now a couple of hundred meters from the designated nuclear dump site. He unlatches the door and jumps out of the fire brigade; he rolls over on the ground, takes out his gun, and takes aim at the tanker. He is poised to ignite the tanker, his finger hovering over the trigger. But before he can pull the trigger, Drago's jeep runs him over with brute force. Drago's task is half finished though, he throttles the jeep towards the Fire Brigade, now moving on its own accord towards the nuclear dump site. He closes in, moving towards the left side of the truck, and he matches up with the speed of the moving fire truck. The nuclear dump site is now just a few meters away. Drago makes a dare devil attempt lunging at the truck. He gets into the cabin of the truck and slams the brake. The truck skids sideways, goes off balance. Drago continues holding onto the steering wheel, but releases the breaks momentarily, to shift the center of gravity, and then slams it again, causing the truck to regain it's lost balance and comes to a grinding halt. Drago's heart beats intensely. His torn shirt exposes the numerous battle scars he has gathered throughout his years.

Drago gets off the truck exhausted, what he does not know is that, the Fire Brigade Driver had been run over, but he was still alive, he crawls back to the gun, which fell off his hands in the hit and run, and he takes the aim again, at the Petrol Tanker. Drago is in his gun's crosshairs, but he would deal with him later. First, he needs to blow the truck, he shifts his gaze towards the truck, his hand follows with the gun in tow. He is about to pull the trigger, when a couple of gunshots are fired, a couple of bullets pierce through his head, silencing him forever. Drago also takes notice of these gun shots. As he walks closer to the slain terrorist, he recognizes their interceptor jeep on the side, and Roma still holding her gun over the terrorist. It appears she shot him point blank.

The BARC Campus is surrounded by a tableau of destruction and despair as the aftermath of the deadly encounter unfolds. The lifeless bodies of the terrorists lie strewn across the ground, their masks of deceit torn, and alongside them are a couple of CISF men, who also meet their untimely end. Caregivers tenderly provide care to the other wounded CISF personnel, while transporting some others to the hospital. The remaining CISF men secure the perimeter once again. The real fire brigades finally arrive on the scene, and they administer quick action to control the fire caused by the explosion.

The BARC staff, is out on the campus by now, and they help their subordinates in all possible ways to restore order. The CISF Chief, BARC Chief, and the young scientist Ramnathan surround Drago, as he looks at the bodies of the slain terrorists. Their bodies have been impaired severely. Drago wonders if these men include the three men he had seen in the photographs. Ramnathan, looks at the bodies of terrorists. Still shivering with fear, he adds, "Today, we are alive only because of you. Thank you very much sir. "Drago, however, is least bothered. He remains vigilant. He is currently assessing the surroundings and glances once more at the immobilized petrol tanker near the dump site. While looking around, his attention is caught by Karthika, who is getting her wounds nursed, the sound of the blast still echoing in her ears. Karthika, aka Fatima, appears to be frantic. Roma is trying to calm her down. Drago catches their **tête-à-tête.** midway.

Roma's voice sounds like a soothing balm amidst the turmoil. "Your son Rizwan will be alright, calm down, calm down, " she reassures Karthika, her words laced with empathy.

Karthika remains unconvinced, her fear palpable, shaking her head, she whispers, "They are very dangerous. "Roma furrows her brows. "They are dead now," she counters, gesturing towards the lifeless bodies of the terrorists. Karthika, shakes her head, frantically.

Drago takes her by her arm and nears the dead bodies of the 4 slain terrorists. "Can you recognize, anyone of them? "His voice is firm yet gentle. Karthika's gaze sweeps over the corpses, her expression a mask of anguish. "No .....there are at least 3 more of them I know of and that includes my husband Sadiq. "

Roma produces a picture of three suspects, holding it out for Karthika's inspection. With a trembling hand, Karthika points towards Sadiq's image, her voice trembling with recognition.

" Yes, this is Sadiq, and the other two, they had come to our house at Murugan Chawl, Bandra, a couple of days earlier," she confirms, her words laden with dread.

Drago's frustration bubbles to the surface, his forehead creased with concern. " Ovaise Sheikh, has also still not surfaced. We are missing something, " he mutters, his mind racing to fill in the gaps.

Drago turns to Roma, who appears to be equally perplexed, their shared uncertainty hanging heavy between them. Drago's gaze drifts across the vast expanse of the campus. The sea shimmers in the distance, the buildings looming like silent sentinels.

And then, amidst the chaos, his eyes alight upon a towering figure – the huge life-size poster of the Prime Minister adorning one building. Beneath the familiar visage, a tagline gleams in bold letters: "*Me Yetoy*- I am coming"

A spark of realization ignites within Drago's mind, a thread of connection weaving its way through the tangled web of mystery.

Drago revisits from his memory the threat analysis estimation report he had presented after the initial survey of the BARC, just 2-3 days earlier. "A powerful blast of reasonable magnitude can trigger radioactivity. The fire could then spread to Dhruv and Cirus reactors, and cause mayhem." He had proclaimed.

Drago glanced at the stranded Fire Brigade, brimming with petrol. Indeed, it appeared to him as a ticking time bomb, a potential ignition source for the nuclear dumpsite, but would it create enough pressure to trigger a fusion or fission reaction? He contemplated, the answer came to him within seconds. He looked at Roma, "One petrol tanker would not have caused enough damage. They would at least need 3-4 petrol tankers exploding simultaneously to make a considerable impact at the dumpsite, and use it as a tinder, to blow up BARC. "Drago declared. Roma nods assertively." And amid this show down, Ovaise Sheikh had still not surfaced. "Roma's analytical mind presented a different but connected perspective to the threat scenario unfolding in front of them. "Does this mean that this blow up was just a distraction? Does it mean it is a part of a bigger, more vicious plan at play?" She ponders over the preposition.

Drago grows weary of Roma's analysis. A worried expression is visible on his face. He knows they have already been outplayed, and just then, Munir calls him. He puts the call on speakerphone so even Roma can listen. Munir appears extremely anxious. Prime Minister was supposed to finish the rally at the Bandra Kurla Complex and head to the airport, but suddenly his entourage took a detour and is now headed towards the old city. I don't know what is happening exactly, but there seems to be more to the story. I will keep you updated."

Munir hangs up the phone. Drago wonders, he looks at Roma, then his eyes fall on the life-size poster of PM fluttering on the nearby building, once again. His mind races in a tizzy. The Prime Minister was an unpredictable figure. Eight years earlier, he had made another such out of schedule visit and landed in Lahore for a meeting with his Pakistani counterpart.

This risky but unprecedented move had shocked the defence fraternity across the world, but this daring move had also emboldened his position in world politics. Back at home, he had laid the foundation for what would be later perceived as the image of decisive governance. From initially making a pitch for the PM's seat with the tag line *"Ab ki Bar PM Sarkar"* to consolidating his power in second term with the slogan *"Fir ek Baar PM Sarkar"* he was now hailed as a hero of the masses across India, for whom people said, *" PM hai to Mumkin Hai"*

PM had taken more such last-minute detours, and Drago thought it could be a similar situation. However, he couldn't help but wonder if this all was part of a larger plan for - Quadath-Ut-Allah.

Chapter 20

Lal Bagh Cha Raja

29 September, 2023

1500 hrs

The Ganpati Pandals set up by various Sarvajanik Ganeshotsav Mandals in Mumbai and other places in the State of Maharashtra attract millions of devotees during the 10-day Ganesh Chaturthi festivities. Amidst the plethora of Ganpati Mandals, Lal Bagh of Mumbai is in the class of its own. Lal Bagh is one of the oldest and the most popular mandals in the metropolis, but it is the magnetism of the Bappa as the wish fulfilling *Lal Bagh Cha Raja*, which attracts around one crore devotees during the 10 days of Ganesh Chaturthi festival. From the biggest film stars to sports personalities and politicians, everyone lines up to seek the blessings of the Bappa, and this time, with the elections round the corner, even the Prime Minister could not resist the charm of *Lal Bagh Cha Raja*.

The grandeur of *Lal Bagh Cha Raja* during Ganesh Chaturthi is a spectacle to behold. Picture this: towering arches adorned with intricate decorations, which extend across a few hundred meters. Shimmering lights casting a magical glow, and the air thick with the scent of burning incense and flowers. As you step into the pandal, the vibrant colors, the rhythmic beats of traditional musical accompaniments, and the fervent chants of devotees overwhelm your senses. To add to the grandeur, every inch of the pandal showcases meticulous craftsmanship, honoring Lord Ganesha with elaborate themes and motifs that blend tradition and innovation.

As the PM's convoy of cars arrived at *Lal Bagh Cha Raja*, an air of anticipation swept through the crowd. Police personnel sprang into action, their voices crackling through walkie-talkies as they directed the flow of traffic. As the VIP convoy entered for Bappa's darshan, the devotees whispered to each other and exchanged curious glances.

Inside the third car of the PM's entourage, Munir engaged in conversation with Drago over the phone. Stepping out of the vehicle, Munir's eyes beheld the splendour of Lal Bagh, the iconic Ganpati Pandal of Mumbai, stretching before him. "Drago, we have arrived at this huge pandal in the heart of the city. "Munir's voice crackled through the phone.

As the PM emerged from his car, enveloped by the SPG-Special Protection Group, he raised his hand in acknowledgment to the crowd. A surge of excitement rippled through the devotees. The fervent cry of "*Ganpati Bappa Morya*" echoed through the air. With folded hands, the PM also joined the chorus. Subsequently, he raised the slogan, "*Bharat Mata ki Jai.*". This was only the beginning. For the next few moments, the crowd reciprocated with a resounding response, alternating between the chants of "*Ganpati Bappa Morya*" and "*Bharat Mata ki Jai.*" The chants grew louder and louder with every passing second.

Amidst the deafening noise, Munir had to step away on the side, to continue talking with Drago "This stop over for Ganesh Darshan was not a part of PM's itinerary," Munir continued, his tone reflecting a mix of surprise and admiration. "But the PM was insistent – that he couldn't leave Mumbai without seeking Bappa's blessings." "And for that, there cannot be a better place than *Lal Bagh Cha Raja*, "Drago completes Munir's sentence.

His response baffles Munir. He scans through the bustling surroundings of *Lal Bagh Cha Raja*, searching for Drago amidst the throngs of people. "Are you already at the *Lal Bagh Cha Raja*? " Munir anticipates, his voice echoes through the phone. From his vantage point, he could see snipers strategically positioned, forming a protective shield around the PM, but Drago was not in sight.

"No, I am not there yet, but I have some bad news to share with you. "Drago's voice crackled with urgency over the line.

As Munir listened intently, Drago recounted the recent events at BARC, the visuals playing out in Munir's mind like a fast-paced film.

The blast at BARC had sent shockwaves through the security apparatus, threatening to unravel into a major disaster. Terrorists, armed with a petrol tanker, posed a grave threat to the facility, but Drago and the CISF averted a catastrophe through quick thinking and decisive action.

Among the chaos, Karthika's keen eye had identified three terror suspects from the photo they had received earlier from the ISIS stronghold in Mosul, Syria. One of them was Sadiq, her husband, their images captured and displayed alongside Ovaise's photograph. All these men were still missing in action. Munir realizes that the pieces of the puzzle were finally falling into place, but the picture still appeared incomplete, especially with Ovaise at large.

Inside the bustling halls of *Lal Bagh Cha Raja*, the Prime Minister made his way towards the revered Ganpati Idol for Mukh Darshan. Munir followed closely behind, his mind preoccupied with the ongoing conversation over the phone.

Meanwhile, back at the BARC compound, CISF personnel worked frantically to maintain order. Four terrorists lay motionless, their sinister plans thwarted. Roma, amidst the commotion, engaged in a tense conversation with the command centre, the mobiles of the slain terrorists were placed in front of her. She is focused on extracting vital information from the terrorists' mobile phones.

In the midst of these events, Drago paced restlessly within the confines of the BARC compound. His voice crackled with urgency as he relayed his concerns to Munir, over the phone. "Sir, I believe the BARC was never their intended target. This was a diversionary tactic to keep us distracted." Drago's words were laced with a sense of foreboding."I think the actual target is the Prime Minister."

PM, leads his way to the *Lal Bagh Cha Raja* idol with a handful of flowers, and the magnanimous idol of *Lal Bagh Cha Raja* is visible in the distance. The SPG group is surrounding him and at the fag end is Munir. Munir's disbelief was palpable. He excuses himself into a corner and responds, "Do you even realize what you're suggesting? The Prime Minister's security is impenetrable. He is one of the most heavily protected persons on the planet "

Munir watches the elaborate layers of security surrounding the Prime Minister as he speaks, "PM's convoy has armoured

BMW 7 series Sedan, 6 BMW X5 and 1 Mercedes Benz Ambulance, with more than a dozen vehicles, other than a Tata Safari Jammer."

Drago is pacing up and down at BARC Campus, desperately trying to make his case and as he speaks, his words paint a picture of PM's security arrangements." Sir, I know there is a group of 100 commandos from the SPG-Special Protection Group. Whether PM's car is attacked by assault rifles like AK-47 or enemy throws hand grenades at the vehicle, our PM will be still safe inside his car. I am aware of that ....I have read all the paperwork. "

Drago's unease persisted. Despite all the security measures, I can't shake the feeling that his life is at risk.

Munir's scepticism was evident over the phone. "You have a feeling, Drago. Have you lost your mind ? This is not the time to pronounce your conspiracy theories."

Drago, continues to argue with Munir. In the background at the BARC site, the rescue operations are almost coming to a closure. The last few wounded men are getting medical help from the Doctors and medical staff.

"Sir, if we had suspicions earlier, we could have advised against the PM's rally. But according to me, Ovaise deliberately waited until the PM came to Mumbai. He knew that once the PM is amidst the civilians, the extraction will become that much more difficult. "

Observing the Prime Minister's interactions within the pandal, Munir grappled with Drago's assertions. "History tells us that most VIP assassinations occur in public spaces, during rallies." Drago emphasized and remained steadfast. "I know I don't have any substantial proof, but my instincts are telling me..."

Drago notices Roma waving at him, even as he continues to speak on the phone. Drago walks towards Roma. Meanwhile, Munir's tone over the phone,hardens with resolve, " Is this the best you can come up with? You know very well that we cannot plan a counter based on your hunch .... I know you can do better than this." Drago feels the pinch. He knows Munir is being reasonable. Drago is with Roma. They are near one of the wounded men. He is injured, and the doctors have bandaged him, but it doesn't look like he will make it.

The CISF man is trying to speak, but he is barely audible. The bullet wound around his neck makes it harder for him to speak. Drago feels concerned. The flailing hands of the soldier remind him of Milind's final moments, just 24 hours earlier.

As Drago gets sucked into the past, Milind's final moments reverberate through his mind, like an auto playback on a constant loop. Munir's voice drowns on him, and the moment of perceived blindness triggers within Drago's being.

FLASHBACK

The moment of Milind's death plays out in front of Drago's eyes, but this time in slow motion. Milind is saying something in his dying moments, while pointing towards his bag." *Plan kuch aur hai...*" Milind blurts out in pain. Drago's attention veers towards Milind, he had been pointing towards his bag, with the DVD of the film "Padmavat", peeping out of it.

Munir, who had been holding onto the phone, incessantly tries to draw Drago's attention. "Dheeraj, Dheeraj... are you there? Can you here me? "Munir's voice eventually lets Drago to snap out of his reverie. A sense of realization has dawned upon Drago. "I will have to call you back sir," he hangs up without waiting for a response. Milind's last words, *"Plan kuch aur hai,"* had caught Drago's attention.

Chapter 21

Pereceived Blindness

Ovaise sat in the car, his car headed towards the next destination. He watched the streets of Mumbai whiz by in a blur, his attention constantly drawn to the notifications on his phone. His fingers tapped impatiently on the screen, seeking information, answers, anything to make sense of the actions he had triggered at the BARC.

His eyes momentarily drifted to the outside world as the car moved steadily ahead. In the distance, a billboard stands, proudly displaying the letters “Chhatrapati Shivaji International Airport,” a recognizable sight in the busy city. The arrow points right, urging travellers towards their respective departure sites at Terminal T1 and T2.

Ovaise’s car continues going straight, on the Western Express way, while he glances at the right side underpass, leading towards the airport. His phone emits a sudden beep, announcing the arrival of a news alert. With a sense of trepidation, he taps on the notification, revealing the headline: “Laboratory Accident at BARC.” Ovaise’s eyes dilate momentarily to focus once again on the news piece, his mind racing to comprehend the outcome. Ovaise looks in disbelief. He clicks the link to open the live feed of the news channel. The News Reporter briefly talks about the laboratory accident, and then immediately switches to a Breaking News update. "PM's surprise visit at *Lal Bagh Cha Raja.*"

A wave of confusion washes over Ovaise as he watches live images of the Prime Minister amidst a throng of devotees, his figure illuminated by the fervent chants of his supporters chanting *"Ganpati Bappa Morya"*, *"Bharat Mata Ki Jay"* Riaz, Ovaise's geeky companion in the car, also takes notice of the news feed with curiosity. He glanced at Ovaise with concern, sensing the turmoil brewing within his boss. Despite the unpredictable circumstances, Ovaise's determination stayed firm.

With the advent of 24-hour news channels and digital platforms, access to timely and relevant information had never been more widespread and instantaneous. Whether it's breaking news, in-depth analysis, or investigative reports, the breadth and depth of coverage offered by news channels revolutionized the way people consumed information.

The news platforms had thus transformed into a vital pillar of society that continued to shape opinions, drive conversations, and inspire action across the nation. One such newsroom of NEWS BHARAT, helmed by anchor Abhivyanajana Mishra, buzzed with activity. She sat at the forefront, flanked by a panel of experts and political party representatives, engaged in a heated discussion about the Prime Minister's surprise visit to *Lal Bagh Cha Raja.*

"We have information from our sources that the Prime Minister was scheduled to head for the Mumbai Airport and fly out of the city after addressing the public rally at Bandra Kurla Complex. Hence, Prime Minister's unscheduled visit at *Lal Bagh Cha Raja* during the Ganesha Chaturthi only implies one thing-Vote Bank Politics. "The anchor's voice reverberated through the room, commanding attention as she dissected the unfolding political manoeuvres before them.

"The ruling party could not secure the majority on its own in the General Elections. They have lost 3 state elections in a row. So, this last-minute drama of visiting "*Lal Bagh Cha Raja*" is nothing more than a political stunt. "The political analyst, who was also a paid actor of the opposition party, emphasized dramatically. "It gives out a clear message that the ruling party wants to win the upcoming Maharashtra State Elections at any cost."

"Or you can also look at this way, that like millions and millions of Bappa's devotees, our Prime Minister is also a devout Ganesh Bhakt" The ruling party spokesperson interjected, "I mean, how can you come to Mumbai during Ganesha Chaturthi celebrations, and leave the city without seeking the blessing of the Vighnaharta- Ganpati Bappa. "Offering a different perspective on the Prime Minister's visit, he highlighted the cultural and spiritual significance of seeking Lord Ganesha's blessings during the auspicious occasion of Ganesh Chaturthi.

That is an interesting point of view, the anchor chimes in, "We are amid this very engrossing debate on the Prime Minister's surprise visit to *Lal Bagh Cha Raja,* but most importantly, we would like to know what is viewers, opinion on this. Type A and SMS to us on 56872- If you think it is a political stunt, like the opposition claims or Type B and SMS to us on 56872-If you think the Prime Minister visited *Lal Bagh Cha Raja* out of devotion."

The debate raged on. Each voice added a layer of complexity to the unfolding narrative.

Meanwhile, Ovaise's car came to a halt outside the towering TV 365 Channel Building on the Western Expressway, at Vile Parle (East) near the airport, in the western suburbs of Mumbai. He finally tears his gaze away from the news feed on his phone, even as he gets out of the car. A reassuring smile graces his lips, despite the uncertainty that looms ahead. He looks at the Ganpati Bappa Idol from the light equipment godown, now mounted on the truck, at the parking facility of the TV 365 Building.

"*Huzoor,* Mr. Prime Minister has headed out somewhere else altogether. What do we do now? " Riyaz, his geeky accomplice, questions Ovaise. "Let him do whatever he wants to. Today, not even this Bappa can save him from meeting his end. "

Determined, Ovaise is, ready to face whatever challenges lie in store. But before he can make his next move, a tap on his shoulder interrupts his train of thought. It's Geetika, the Creative Producer, her expression a mix of urgency and concern. "Nicolas, sir, hurry up please, we are already behind schedule."

Ovaise stretches his hands and legs, now switching his tonality to that of the French man Nicolas, he acknowledges Geetika's words with a nod of understanding." I know, I know, but nothing to worry, Geetika, we will be back on track in no time. I always have a Plan B, and we will improvise... *Ganapati Bappa Morya.*"

The whole crew around him looks enthused by the *Ganapati Bappa Morya,* slogan and they too, scream in unison, in their heart of hearts though, they knew it was a battle cry, and the moment they had all waited for over months, had finally started to unfold.

BARC, Chembur, Mumbai

29 September, 2023

1530 hrs

Inside the conference room, which had been temporarily converted into the situation room. Roma, along with a team of analysts, meticulously scrutinized the data retrieved from the mobile phones of the slain terrorists. Each piece of information was like a fragment of a puzzle, waiting to be pieced together to reveal the bigger picture. With Roma's keen eye and the analysts' technical expertise, they were determined to unearth any hidden connections that could shed light on the recent attacks.

Drago's abrupt entrance broke their concentration. His face showed a sense of urgency as he handed them a DVD discovered in Milind's belongings. The room fell silent as Drago emptied another bag filled with DVDs onto the table. The significance of the discovery was unclear to everyone present in the room.

Drago flashed the DVD of Padmavat to everyone, announcing that he found this DVD with Milind, his voice carrying a weight of importance. "Milind was trying to tell us something." Drago added.

Drago then pointed at the entire bag of DVDs and continued, "This was retrieved from the suspect, whom we chased down near the Jehangir Art Gallery. Apparently, he was in the business of pirating film DVDs. Now, since the suspect is in a coma, it is left to us to make the connection? "

While thinking about the DVDs, Roma suddenly had a realization. With a sense of purpose, she swiftly moved to another workstation, instructing the operators to retrieve specific footage of Ovaise and Aarif's last interactions.

"Get the meeting point footage of Ovaise Sheikh and Aarif, from Goregaon East." Roma commanded, her voice tinged with determination.

The operator quickly types in the keywords and the footage of Ovaise and Aarif, where Ovaise was dropped off at a point in Goregaon East, shows up on screen. Roma stops the video at a precise point. It is indeed another DVD, but the image is blurry. Roma orders to upscale the CCTV grab. Just then, the operator, notices an existing sub-folder created by Milind. He immediately calls upon Roma and clicks open the folder. An upscale image of the CCTV grab is already present. In the image, Aarif is seen giving to Ovaise, a DVD of the Sanjay Leela Bhansali film - Black.

Roma's mind raced as she connected the dots. Milind had already pursued this lead and either he had already cracked the mystery, or he died in the pursuit of solving it. Tragically, he was killed before he had the chance to share the information with anyone.

Roma's intuition guided her towards a startling understanding. Milind was in possession of the DVD, 'Padmavat' and the DVD exchanged between Aarif and Ovaise was titled,'Black'. They both were made by the same filmmaker- Sanjay Leela Bhansali. Could there be a connection? She wonders. She scrambles across the stack of DVDs emptied on the desk. She instructs the team to look for DVDs, which had Sanjay Leela Bhansali film on it.

In the next few seconds, 4 DVDs of SLB Films are scavenged out from the spread. Roma picks up the DVDs and hands it over to the analysts." Check all these DVDs and see if you find something indifferent. "Roma instructs.

Drago realizes Roma is stretching way too much, she is in pain but she is not showing it. Despite the urgency of their task, he couldn't help but feel a sense of admiration for Roma's unwavering determination and sharp intellect. Drago just pushes a chair towards her. Roma acknowledges the gesture.

Minutes later, an analyst makes a breakthrough, discovering an anomaly in one of the DVDs—"Right towards the end, after the titles roll, Pics of Mumbai city's road map, blueprint of BARC and other similar images are showing up. "The analyst reveals. Roma and Drago watch the embedded sequence of photos closely. Drago senses a breakthrough and urges immediate action: "Inspect all four DVDs and let's see what we can uncover."

In another DVD, an embedded sequence of photos and propaganda material related to the BARC and Mumbai are found. The room fell silent as the gravity of the discovery sank in.

With meticulous precision, the analysts compile the data and relay it on the big screen. Each DVD had different information embedded in them. Drago speaks his mind, as he and Roma watch the data unfold. "Clearly they have been using these DVDs to circulate information amongst their network, and it seems they adopted a piecemeal approach?" Roma iterates for everyone, "Piece meal approach means the person receives only selected pieces of information, pertaining to the specific tasks allotted to them, on a need to know basis. Correct? " Drago nods. "Yes, and this also means that they are probably working with a much wider net of people than we can imagine." "Sleeper cells…it has to be the sleeper cells." Roma retorts.

At about that time, the info from Padmavat DVD- the last one in the lot gets uploaded. The DVD has PM's photos, photos of his convoy, the pre -approved route from Airport to BKC and back to the airport. Drago's expressions becomes serious. As Drago contemplates the implications of their findings, Roma's voice cuts through the silence, her words laced with uncertainty, yet tinged with resolve.

"Ovaise has proved to be a genius mastermind," she remarks, her gaze fixed on the screen.

Leaving the Situation Monitoring Room, Drago strode purposefully through the corridor, his mind racing with various permutations, combinations of their discovery. Roma followed closely behind, eager to discuss and understand the full extent of what they had stumbled upon.

"Do you know why a magician is always accompanied by an extremely good looking assistant?" Drago asks Roma. Roma is thrown off the hook by Drago's irrelevant question. "No, but why? " she shoots back, as Drago enters the weapons room.

A variety of rifles, automatic machine guns, and ammunitions are stacked up in the room. Drago wears a harness, chooses a Glock-17, tests its mechanism, while talking to Roma. "Good looking assistants serve as a useful distraction for the magician performing the show. "Roma still cannot connect the dots. "What the hell are you even talking about?" she snaps. "BARC attack was a useful distraction,the actual target is the Prime Minister. "Drago declares his voice is now filled with conviction.

Roma watched in astonishment, her mind reeling from the revelation, Drago meanwhile fills his harness with the ammunition and says "Ovaise is the magician, BARC was a useful distraction, PM's assassination is the result of this whole act, but I still cannot figure out what is the magic trick here. "

"Magic trick?" Roma asks for clarification. "Meaning we still don't know from where the attack on PM is going to come from and in what way? "Drago shakes his head in disbelief, continues to test the mechanism of another Glock-17 gun, relying on his muscle memory honed over years of practice, and then hands the gun over to Roma. "You are going to need this." Roma is astonished at Drago's clarity of thought. She is about to take the gun when Drago pulls the gun back. "But you don't have to do this, given your pregnancy. "Drago hints at Roma's baby bump. "Whether it is he or she, my kid will be a Gorkha someday, just like my father was and I am. We will endure this and more, we are cut for situations like these. "Roma pulls the gun firmly from Drago's hands "Besides, you are forgetting , that if it wasn't for me,that tanker might have still exploded, and even you might have been injured. "Roma adds. Drago remembers how Roma had taken down the terrorist point blank, before he could fire at the petrol tanker. His eyes are filled with admiration, " It's always an honour to fight alongside a Gorkha." Drago salutes her as they walk away.

Chapter 22
Plan B

Ovaise is staring intensely at the MANPAD's arrowhead. The wooden box housing the deadly weapon lay partially open, among other shooting equipment strewn across the rooftop. Sadiq stands next to Ovaise, he informs him with a smile that all the equipment had been safely transported on the terrace of the TV 365 Building. Ovaise looks satisfied. Meanwhile, the Creative Producer, Geetika, calls for him at the top of her voice. The matter seems to be urgent. Ovaise, however, is too busy thinking about the terror he is about to unleash. Sadiq elbows him, drawing his attention towards Geetika. Ovaise pushes the cover of MANPAD back on, and heads towards Geetika.

"Nicolas is a busy man today, but he is always at your service, Mademoiselle," Ovaise announces as he joins the remainder of the crew seated with Geetika. Geetika brings out her to do list, that contains a plethora of creative shots, which she wants to take from the rooftop to cover the Ganpati Visarjan festivities. She looks at her watch. It is 3:45 PM, "The Ganesh-Gauri Visarjan of Ganesh Chaturthi, should begin anytime now. Ganpati idols will begin their final journey leading to Juhu Chowpaty. "She speaks, pointing to the road ahead of their building and draws an imaginary line with her hand leading to Juhu Chowpaty, visible in the distance.

"Look Nicolas, I had to write a lot of mails, to procure permission for this one day of shoot, although it is our own terrace building. Let's execute our plans well, so that we get all the shots that we want for the documentary," Geetika requests with sincerity. Nicolas puts his hand on her shoulders and calms her down. "Relax Geetika, we have handled shoots of bigger magnitude than this. You just wait and watch , as we weave the magic. " Despite his mind being preoccupied with other matters, he remained outwardly engaged. His facade as a member of the film crew was firmly in place.

Parel, Mumbai

29 September, 2023
1550 hrs

The streets of Mumbai bustled with activity as Mumbaikars prepared for the Ganesh-Gauri Visarjan. Police officers blew their whistles, attempting to manage the flow of traffic amidst diversions and road closures, imposed for the Visarjan procession. Constable Patil, with his commanding presence, guided vehicles through the intricate streets.

Amid the chaotic scene, a Ganpati Idol stood proudly, gradually being prepared for the Visarjan proceedings. The rhythmic beats of Nashik Dhol players echoed in the background, adding to the festive ambiance of the occasion. At another place further ahead, a truck loaded with huge speakers and a DJ console was being prepped for the musical extravaganza. As the

DJ tested his music system, young kids rehearsed their dance steps to the beats. Everyone looked excited, for Bappa's Visarjan journey from the pandal to the sea.

Meanwhile, Drago's car hurtled towards Parel, the place where *Lal Bagh Cha Raja* was stationed. Due to the special forces tag on their interceptor car, they smoothly sailed through with minimal traffic on the road. But he could already see other vehicles getting funnelled into single rows for better movement of Ganesha Visarjan traffic. His subordinate, Vikas Mhatre, a junior analyst like Milind, skilfully manoeuvred the car. Taking a turn a few hundred meters ahead, would then lead them to *Lal Bagh Cha Raja*.

Their expressions were inscrutable, hinting at the weight of their mission amid the celebratory atmosphere. Drago's attention was drawn to an under-construction site along the way, marked by a signboard proclaiming "Mumbai Metro-Work Under Progress." Drago jogged his memory and double checked with Vikas. "Isn't this the part of the Mumbai Underground Metro Line connecting the old town and suburbs? "Vikas responded promptly, "Yes Sir, that is correct. It's a 30-kilometer long underground network, connecting different parts of the city "

Drago's car navigates through the last league of traffic, witnessing devotees making their way on foot to *Lal Bagh Cha Raja* for darshan. The long queues for darshan could sometimes stretch for 10-12 hours, but the faithful continue to wait with a smile on their lips and hope in their hearts. As Drago's car approached the main entrance of *Lal Bagh Cha Raja*, he saw two enormous TV screens broadcasting live feeds of Ganpati Bappa at Lal Bagh. Hundreds of devotees stood in reverence, their hands folded in a prayer.

News Bharat Studio, Lower Parel, Mumbai

29 September, 2023

1555 hrs

Meanwhile, in another part of the city, a live feed showcasing the Prime Minister's visit to *Lal Bagh Cha Raja* played on one screen. Inside the bustling newsroom of the news channel office of NEWS BHARAT in Lower Parel. Abhivyanjana Mishra - The news anchor, previously engaged in covering the PM's surprise visit, now collaborated with her video editor on a story titled *"PM aur Protocol."* She is still deciding upon her voice over lines for the piece. "The Prime Minister of our country loves breaking protocols without understanding what a security nightmare it can actually turn into. Earlier he had pulled off something similar when he landed in Lahore, Pakistan unannounced, and now ......" Before she can finish her lines, she is interrupted by her editor, broaching the topic with a hint of caution, "Madam, landing in Lahore, was part of politics, but *Lal Bagh Cha Raja* is a matter of faith. How can we raise questions about someone's faith? And also he is the Prime Minister of the country? "The editor questioned, mindful of the sensitivities involved.

"Look my job is to raise questions, and I suggest you, should also stick to your job, which at this time is to edit the video... 'PM aur Protocol!!!' We need to be on air with this story in the next hour. *Waqt nahin hai hamare paas,"* Abhivyanjana, replied firmly, emphasizing the urgency of the situation.

Video editor, looked on with a blank face, meanwhile Abhivyanjana's phone rings. She is in a dilemma, whether to take the call or focus on the story. Then her experience triggers her response. In her 8 years of TV Journalism, she had realized that any call could be a potential lead to breaking news. She signals the editor to begin work and moves away to receive the call.

"Hello!" She answers, her voice expectant. But there is no response for a while, prompting her to inquire further. "*Kuch bologe bhi... ya sirf awaaz sunn ni hai....*"

"BARC mein jo hua, wo ek laboratory accident nahin tha. Terrorist Attack tha," a voice interrupted, sending a jolt of adrenaline rush through Abhivyanjana.

Alert and focused, she rushed to the Editor-in-Chief's cabin, quickly putting her phone on speaker as she gestured for the Editor-in-Chief's attention.

"*Aee bewde... aaj visarjan se pehle hi sharab pi rakhi hai kya*?," she questioned tersely, her mind already racing with the implications of the call.

Ovaise, is listening to Abhivyanjana Mishra, besides him is the camera crew prepping for a shot on the terrace of the TV 365 Building. Ovaise returns to his position beside the MANPAD. Taking a sip of water from his bottle, he responds. " I don't drink as such, but we are going to celebrate tonight. *Terrorist Attack samajhti ho.* That happened at BARC and now Mumbai's heart is going to be pounded, in the next few minutes- *Rok sako toh rok lo*," Ovaise remarked cryptically, his words laden with an ominous intent.

Inside the Editor-in-Chief's cabin, at NEWS BHARAT, tension hung thick in the air as Abhivyanjana confronted the shocking revelation delivered over the phone." Why should I believe you?" Abhivyanjana questioned, her voice tinged with disbelief.

Ovaise's response was curt and filled with veiled menace. *"Thik hai, fir dhamake... ka intezaar kar lijiye. Tab tak mein kisi aur news channel se baat kar leta hoon."*

"N-No no no, wait wait. *Aap kaun baat kar rahe hai?* Who are you? " Abhivynajana stammered, desperation evident in her tone.

But Ovaise's voice on the other end of the line offered no reassurance. *"Jaldi kya hai,* you can read it in tomorrow's newspaper," he retorted before abruptly disconnecting the call.

The Editor-in-Chief and Abhivyanjana exchanged horrified glances. It took just a few moments for them to fully comprehend the gravity of Ovaise's intent. The threat was real, and they grappled with the implications of the call. A sense of urgency permeated the room, signalling the beginning of a race against time.

At *Lal Bagh Cha Raja,* Drago and his RAW Associate made their way through the bustling pandal, flanked by a volunteer from the *Lal Bagh Cha Raja* organizing committee. The sight of long queues of devotees carrying flowers and pooja thalis greeted them. It painted an elaborate picture of devotion and fervour. *"Ye line kuch zyada badi nahin hai*?" Drago remarked to the volunteer, his brow furrowed with concern.

The volunteer, in contrast, responded with a broad smile, "Sir, we had 1.5 crore visitors over the 10 days of Ganesh Chaturthi last year, so at an average there are about 1.4 to 1.5 million visitors every day " Drago draws an estimate "So going by that logic, at this time there must be around 5-6 lakh people in the vicinity "The volunteer, nods acknowledging his estimate.

Drago looks more concerned now. His mind running various permutation combinations, as he looks around in all directions, making broad estimates. In the process Drago's expression darkens as he glances at one of the screens displaying live feed. The Prime Minister was shown holding a pooja ki thali, his presence stirring unease within Drago.

He swiftly dialled Roma, even as the *Lal Bagh Cha Raja* volunteer continued trailing behind him. "Roma, do we have any update from the terrorist's mobile data? " He urged, his voice tinged with urgency.

BARC, Chembur, Mumbai

29 September, 2023

1620 hrs

In the Situation Monitoring Room, Roma stood before the GEO -SPATIAL INTELLIGENCE module of the IIS- Integrated Intelligence System, and the graphical representation of the data retrieved from the terrorist's mobile phones overlaid on it. She continued to work with her team while still pressing the phone to her ears.

"We are close to cracking it. I have also spoken to the defence attaché of the CIA-Middle East, to get whatever more info he can about Ovaise. Also, one more primary observation from the data is that there are at least 8-10 different individuals who were connected to these men. Their locations seem to be scattered all around the city," Roma informed.

"This little side show of Ovaise is going to play out very soon, I think.... We need to move in fast and we need to move in now. Also share the screen grabs of this GEO -Spatial data you have worked on so far," Drago's voice echoed, as Roma acknowledged his directive.

Roma hangs up the phone, sends out the work in progress. GEO -Spatial data files to Drago and addresses her staff. "Ovaise had been off the radar for close to 3 years. Of course, he worked closely with ISIS, but I want you all to find out everything about where he went, and whom did he did meet during this time. "

Lal Bagh Cha Raja, Parel, Mumbai

29 September, 2023
1640 hrs

Back at Lal Bagcha Raja, Drago and Munir convened in the VIP lounge. Drago's subordinate, Vikas, is taking Munir, through the photographs and data retrieved from the DVDs, on his I Pad.

Munir looks at PM's photos, his travel plan, blueprints of the city retrieved from DVD. In the background we can hear the sounds of manjira and dhol getting louder with every passing second. Drago swipes one more time. The next pic on the pad, shows the skyline of Mumbai from a vantage point. No matter how hard they tried, this one photo remained elusive and refused to fit into the puzzle.

"Sir, apart from this photo everything else is clear, and the propaganda material only indicates further that they are targeting the most popular Prime Minister India, has seen over the last 3 decades " Drago concluded, his tone grave.

Munir nodded in agreement, acknowledging the gravity of the situation. "Our current PM is also the most protected PM of the recent times. "He said, trying to find a silver lining in the chaos. "I understand, sir, but our first priority should be to move him away from here, to a designated safe zone. "Drago responded.

Munir, nods in agreement, and as they prepared to leave the secured zone, the sound of manjira and dhol grew louder, a stark contrast to the tension in the air. "It's code Red... get the convoy ready," Munir commanded over the walkie talkie, his voice relaying the urgency of the situation.

Amidst the rhythmic claps and chants of the aarti, Drago and Munir arrive at the main pandal, where the Pujari is seen putting a tilak on Prime Minister's forehead. Chief of PM's Staff, is at the Pandal. The sounds of manjira and other accompaniments transform into the beginning of Aarti. "Sir, we will have to wait for a bit. "Chief of PM's Staff responds politely, pointing towards the Pujari, who is just handing over the puja platter to PM. And the Aarti begins.

The PM begins the Aarti of Ganapati Idol. In the background, thousands of devotees actively participate in the aarti with rhythmic claps. Drago, Munir, and the security team look concerned. Despite the fervent devotion surrounding them, the weight of their mission bore heavily on their minds.

The *Lal Bagh Cha Raja* volunteer, however, remained unperturbed, offering words of reassurance. " Bappa is also known as Vighnaharta- The Destroyer of obstacles. I don't know what matter is concerning you so deeply, but I know for sure that Bappa will definitely help you in your cause and show you the way." The volunteer starts clapping and singing the aarti in unison along with the crowd.

As the devotees eagerly awaited their turn to seek blessings from Ganapati Bappa, the air hummed with anticipation, each moment carrying the weight of uncertainty and possibility. Munir closes his eyes in a quiet prayer. Drago's eyes shut in reverence as he salutes *"Ganpati Bappa Morya,"* He is completely in sync with the rhythmic beats of the dhols and cymbals, and so are his moves and countermoves, taking shape in his mind..

Chapter 23

Boom Boom....

Several Ganpati idols had started their visarjan procession, making their way through the streets towards Juhu Beach for immersion in the sea. The devotees danced to the tunes of dhol and tasha, while some other Ganpati mandals carried an entourage of sound and music equipment, with a DJ at the helm of these musical trucks. Ovaise's team creatively captured this visarjan frenzy from the rooftop of TV 365 Building. Ovaise, however, was busy on the phone. Geetika, who kept a tab on the proceedings, took a note of this.

Positioned among the shooting equipment, Ovaise kept the MANPAD in his line of sight while setting the next phase of the plan in motion. "There is no room for error. "He checks his watch and instructs his henchmen. It is 4: 55 PM.

Ovaise's two men, who are temporarily placed in a dingy apartment, nod in agreement and disconnect the phone with a salutation. *"Takbir"*. Both these men are Sadiq's aides from the ISIS photograph. They align the time on their watch with Ovaise's watch and set it to 4. 55PM.

Parel, Mumbai

29 September, 2023

1656 hrs

Suleiman was dressed in an all-white pants and shirt, which appeared to be weathered over a period. Staring at his reflection in the mirror, he applies a red-colored tilak on his forehead and wears a traditional Gandhi Topi, which had become the identity of the "Marathi Manus" over the years. Iqbal, dressed in a simple chequered shirt and brown baggy pants, helps Suleiman by tying the mauli bangles (red threads). Suleiman, then with extreme caution, picks up a multi layered stainless steel, TIFFIN BOX.

The Tiffin box is taken downstairs and placed on a cycle's rack, along with other meticulously numbered tiffin boxes marked in blue. Suleiman now looks like a complete - Dabbawalla.

In the bustling heart of Mumbai, a remarkable example of teamwork thrives–The Dabbawalas. Dressed in a white outfit and traditional Gandhi Cap, this network of 5000+ Dabbawalas, orchestrate the seamless delivery of thousands of lunchboxes known as 'Dabbas' across the city, and provide the Mumbaikars with home cooked food that is lug between home and office daily. Ovaise was about to use this unique food delivery mechanism of Mumbai, against its very own people.

Suleiman and Iqbal share a hug before going their separate ways. Suleiman, disguised as the dabbawalla, makes his way towards a small Ganpati Pandal, while Iqbal, dressed as a civilian, subtly blends in with the crowd. Iqbal watches Suleiman's movements with a mixture of anticipation and apprehension.

Lal Bagh Cha Raja, Parel, Mumbai

29 September, 2023

1700 hrs

Back at *Lal Bagh Cha Raja,* the Prime Minister continues to perform the Aarti. Drago, his security detail, stands alert, his gaze flickering across the multitude of the crowd, searching for any signs of suspicious behaviour.

The atmosphere crackles with tension, the air heavy with the weight of impending events. Prime Minister's every gesture seems amplified, his presence a beacon amidst the fervor of the religious celebration.

Meanwhile, in the lane adjacent to Lal Bagh. The vibrant beats of the Nashik Dhol resonate through the air, punctuating the excitement building up around the pandals as visarjan preparations for some of the Ganapati mandals reach their peak. This pandal is right at the last turn, from the main road, which leads to the *Lal Bagh Cha Raja.* Amidst the hustle and bustle, Suleiman the Dabbawala in disguise comes to a halt near the pandal, his presence catches the attention of Constable Patil.

Constable Patil's brow furrows as he checks his watch. It is 5: 05 PM, a seemingly unusual time for a dabbawalla to be around. Approaching the dabbawala with suspicion etched on his face, he prepares to interrogate him. But the dabbawala, unfazed, reverently folds his hands and closes his eyes in front of the Ganpati Bappa Idol, pretending to be oblivious to Patil's scrutiny.

Meanwhile, back at the Lal Bagh Pandal, the main aarti of Ganapati Bappa has concluded. However, the musical instruments continue to play rhythmically, paving the way for "Karpur Gauram Aarti"-the final phase of the auspicious ritual. Big chunks of camphor are lit in the pooja thali for the -Karpur Gauram Aarti and flowers get distributed amongst the people, as the rhythmic chants gradually pick up pace.

Prime Minister leads the aarti singing "*Karpur Gauram Karuna Vataram, Sansarsaraam Bhujgendraharam.........*" the devotees also sing along, adding to the celebratory devotion. The atmosphere appears to be electric, with the fragrance of flowers filling the air.

Back at the other pandal near the Lal Bagh turn, Suleiman the Dabbawala in disguise realizes that the Police Constable is still standing in front of him. He knows he is in a precarious situation. He folds his hands one more time and then "*Ganpati Bappa Morya...*" he improvises, looking at Constable Patil. As a creature of habit, Patil responds with the same salutation:

"*Ganpati Bappa Morya*" but Patil does not give him a clean chit yet. He interrogates the dabbawalla but slightly differently. "*Kay re aaj khup ushir zala*?" Patil questions him if he was late today, but in Marathi, "*Ho Saheb*?" Suleiman responds like a well-practiced parrot. Suleiman had done his homework, and he had received thorough training. Patil adds to the complexity of the question, "*Dista tasa nasta, mahnunach jag fasta....Gadhva Mama banavtoy naa*? "Patil adds jovially, stating in Marathi "Appearances can be deceiving. Tell me the truth, you are making a fool out of me, aren't you? "Once again, Suleiman responds with a "*Ho saheb ...ho Saheb* "which is an equivalent of a "yes sir" and nods deliberately, even as he slyly glances at his watch.

Patil's suspicion proves to be true. He nods along, then breaks into a laughter, which eventually takes a turn and Patil lands a deafening slap on Suleiman. He holds him by the collar. "Let me add to your knowledge of Marathi," Patil taunts.

Suleiman realizes that his cover is blown. He instinctively pushes Patil and starts running away, abandoning the cycle and the dabbas behind.

Back at the Lal Bagh Pandal. The Ganapati Aarti of "Karpur Gauram" is at a high pitch and arriving at its logical conclusion. The crowd singing along" *Achyutam Keshvam Ramnarayanam, Krishnadamodaram, Vasudevam Hari, Shridharam, Madhavam, Gopika Vallabha, Janaki Nayakam, Ramchandram Bhaje."* At about the same time people in the crowd start receiving news alerts, the back to back mobile notification sounds becomes omnipresent in the pandal, making it impossible to ignore. Drago makes a mental note of this. He instinctively knows something big is about to unfold.

Just outside the Lal Bagh turn, Patil chases Suleiman the Dabbawala in disguise. As Patil watches him escape in the crowded streets, a realization dawns upon him. He then stops in his tracks. He looks back, notices the cycle left behind by the dabbawala. Patil starts walking back to the cycle. He reports on his walkie talkie, informing the team about the suspect in dabbawalla disguise and the abandoned cycle left behind at the Lal Bagh Naka.

Back at the *Lal Bagh Cha Raja,* the aarti has reached a crescendo, with the chants of "*Hare Ram, Hare Ram, Ram Ram Hare Hare, Hare Krishna, Hare Krishna, Krishna Krishna Hare Hare.....Mangalmurti Morya*" The mobile notification continue to pop on people's screens, some of them are already reading the SMS alert. The chatter amongst people grows. Drago and Munir wonder what is happening. Just then Drago's phone vibrates. He reads the News Alert from NEWS BHARAT, "Terror Alert- A terrorist organization has threatened to blow up the heart of Mumbai"

Just outside, near the Lal Bagh Naka, Suleiman and his partner Iqbal, having fled the chaos, converge at a safe distance. Suleiman is still panting, but there is a sense of urgency in his movements. He exchanges a glance with Iqbal and nods. Iqbal swiftly dials a number on his phone. The phone connects, it rings a couple of times, there is a momentary silence and then moments later, a deafening explosion rips through the air as the Dabbawala Cycle rigged with explosives detonates, sending shrapnel and debris flying in all directions.

Pandemonium reigns supreme. Constable Patil lies wounded on the ground, his blood staining the pavement beneath him. Nearby, the once lively scene of Visarjan proceedings is now a grim tableau of devastation. Civilians, including the Nashik Dhol players, sprawled lifeless amidst the wreckage.

At the *Lal Bagh Cha Raja* Pandal, everyone hears the deafening sound of the blast nearby. Chaos ensues, as more than 500,000 thousand devotees gathered at the *Lal Bagh Cha Raja* run amuck in search of safety.

Amidst the cacophony of screams and sirens, the Prime Minister's SPG security team, led by Munir and Drago, springs into action. With precision and determination, they form a protective shield around the Prime Minister, swiftly ushering him away from the main idol of *Lal Bag Cha Raja*.

Meanwhile, police vans start converging at the blast site, from all directions, their flashing lights illuminating the chaos that continues to unfold just a few meters away from the revered *Lal Bagh Cha Raja*. Before law enforcement can fully comprehend the situation, Suleiman and his accomplice emerge from the shadows, launching a ruthless assault on one of the police vans stationed at the far end of the blast site.

In a swift and calculated manoeuvre, the terrorists overpower the van's driver, swiftly silencing him with a brutal slit to the throat. His lifeless body is callously discarded at the rear of the van, as the terrorists seize control, commandeering the vehicle with chilling efficiency.

Drago, Munir, and the Prime Minister's Chief of Staff gather around a makeshift table in the hastily set up command centre at the VIP lounge of *Lal Bagh Cha Raja*. They spread out a detailed map of Mumbai before them.

Munir gestures confidently as he outlines their strategy. "SPG will establish a 30-meter perimeter from here on to escort the PM to his vehicle."

He marks the designated route on the map, circling the Mayor's residence with a decisive stroke of his pen. "From here, we'll proceed towards Byculla Circle, ensuring the PM's safety en route to the designated safe house - The Mayor's Bungalow."

Drago interjects, his voice tinged with concern. "Sir, this is precisely what Ovaise wants. He's baiting us, testing our response." Taking the Pad from his subordinate Vikas, Drago once again, presents the images they had retrieved from the DVD to reinforce his point. "We've all seen his reconnaissance photos,sir. He's not like Ajmal Kasab, who will fire blindly. He's a strategist. He's a man with a plan," Drago continued.

As they huddle together, the gravity of the situation weighs heavily upon them. "Sir, he knows that taking the PM to a safe house will be our initial move. We can't afford to make that mistake. In all probability, he already knows the safe location." The tension in the room is palpable as they grapple with the adversary's cunning tactics, knowing that every decision could tip the scales, in this high-stakes game, of cat and mouse.

TV 365 Building, Mumbai

29 September, 2023

1715 hrs

Ovaise is seated with his laptop open in front of him. He had already received the call from Suleiman and Iqbal, confirming the blast near *Lal Bagh Cha Raja*. He knows he has done enough to smoke the PM out. The Map of Mumbai from his reconnaissance pics is open in front of him. Ovaise makes another call.

A serene atmosphere envelops the Mayor's Bungalow, where meticulous care is evident in every detail of the garden. Despite the ringing of a phone in the distance, a gardener tends to a rose plant with precise care. Taking his own time, the gardener puts aside the freshly cut rose stem and as he answers the call, he also reveals the bustling activity within the bungalow. "Yes sir, the bouquet is ready," "What about the Biryani?" Ovaise's voice filters out from the gardener's phone.

The gardener glimpses at the chef in the distance. He is diligently preparing the elaborate supper for his potential guests. The gardener and the chef both exchange a knowing smile. "*Ji sahib Biryani bhi taiyaar hai. Agar hamare mehman tashrif laate hai, toh unki puri khatirdari karne ka zimma hamara hai.* "if any of our guests arrive, hospitality will be our utmost priority, the gardener emphasises.

The exchange between Ovaise and the gardener underscores the meticulous planning and attention to detail that characterizes every aspect of Ovaise's operation. As the pieces of his scheme fall into place, the stage is set for the drama to unfold.

Back at the rooftop, Ovaise sits facing his laptop, engrossed in his work, a satisfactory smile emerges on his face. He has finished his call and is about to delve back into his tasks when Geetika, the creative producer of TV 365, approaches him from behind.

"Nicolas, were you speaking in Hindi?" Geetika questions him. Ovaise smiles. *"Yeah, 'thoda thoda'*, -A little bit. Just coordinating with the local production crew. Making sure that our upcoming days of shoot also stay on track." "Yeah, it better be, considering the circumstances." Geetika responds, offering him a Modak from a plateful of Prasad, from their Office Ganpati. Ovaise accepts a Modak graciously.

He swiftly transcends from being Ovaise to Nicolas and then back, as he expresses his urgent need to make a call with a charming smile. Geetika nods understandingly and steps aside. As Ovaise proceeds, he directs his attention to his intricate web of plans unfolding before him. Geetika's smile, however disappears, she had overheard Nicolas, speaking flawless Hindi/Urdu, which was unusual for a foreigner. She has an ominous feeling. Something is odd about Nicolas, she realizes.

Chapter 24
Drago Strikes Back

The *Lal Bagh Cha Raja,* Ganpati Mandal is a scene of chaos. It is a stampede with the 500,000 plus devotees trying to filter out from the area, after the explosion nearby. The security personnel are trying hard to restore order, but the area is just too small and they're far too many people squeezed in. The snipers positioned strategically within *Lal Bag Cha Raja* remain on high alert, but they haven't been able to identify a specific target.

Meanwhile, Munir and Drago, Chief of PM's Staff, flanked by other security heads, stand in earnest discussion at the makeshift command centre in the VIP lounge. The time taken for the impending decision was weighing heavily upon them. The PM had been safely guarded by a ring of SPG commandos around him. Drago, meanwhile, had provided enough evidence to drill a hole in the standard protocol. "What do you suggest?" Munir's inquiry hung in the air.

With a sense of purpose, Drago spreads a blank sheet of paper beside the Map of Mumbai, his pen tracing invisible paths as he pictorially presented the revised plan. "We have 15 vehicles in the Prime Minister's convoy. Our route till the Byculla Circle will remain unchanged," Drago explained, his tone decisive.

He elaborated that at the Byculla Circle, they would divide the convoy into three groups. And each group would be tasked with a specific role in safeguarding the Prime Minister's journey ahead. "We will divide the convoy of 15 cars into groups of 5 cars each. Two groups out of these will be a decoy and head out in two different directions, to send the terrorists on a wild goose chase, while the third group will escort the Prime Minister directly to the airport. "

"Ovaise and his men won't be able to pursue all the fragmented groups, no matter how hard they try. "Drago asserted, his confidence unfaltering. "Before Ovaise figures it out, the Prime Minister will be on his way to the airport, and fly out further for New Delhi."

While some officers nodded in agreement, Munir's dissenting voice pierced the air. "Dividing the convoy poses too great a risk. This way we will compromise PM's security," he argued, his concern palpable. "Our protocols exist for situations like these. We must stick to the protocol and move him to the safe house."

"Sir, maybe you are right. And I hope you are right. But we cannot afford to ignore the signs before us." Drago continued to advocate his version of the solution.

"Drago, I am not as gifted as you are. I am just following protocol. "In a tense exchange, Munir puts his stamp of authority. "*Allah na kare, par agar mein galat nikla, to PM ki suraksha tumhari zimmedari hogi.* Right now I will lead the convoy, aur tum PM ke exact aagewali gaadi mein rahoge." Munir announces.

The decision is made, and PM begins to be escorted into his car, surrounded by the security ring of SPG commandos. The 15 bullet proof and bomb proof cars of PM's convoy were already on a standby, and as soon as the dignitaries filled the designated spots, the convoy starts moving. Leading the convoy as a scout vehicle is a police gypsy, followed by Munir in the lead car. Drago is in the car right before the PM's car.

With the convoy in motion, the city's streets became a labyrinth of uncertainty. Drago's senses heightened as they passed familiar landmarks, each one a potential threat in the intricate dance of security and danger.

Drago notices yet another under construction tunnel passing by. He remembered his junior analyst, Vikas Mhatre's words, when he was reaching *Lal Bag Cha Raja.* He had mentioned that Mumbai's underground metro network was nearing completion, the tunnelling work had been complete. Drago makes a mental note, as they press on towards the Byculla Circle and then onwards to the safe house.

A sense of dread fills the air as a police gypsy escorts the Prime Minister's convoy across the Byculla bridge, with law enforcement clearing the way. On the opposite side of the bridge, traffic is already halted, diverted by a strategically placed police van.

As the convoy draws closer, an ominous truth is revealed— The police van is ostensibly a symbol of security, but this van present on the opposite side of the road, houses Suleiman and Iqbal. After triggering the bomb blast, the two terrorists had taken advantage of the commotion, hi-jacked the police van, and killed the driver. They had changed into the police uniforms and placed themselves strategically with an intent of unleashing chaos.

Alert to their surroundings, the terrorists fix their gaze at a critical juncture of the bridge, which they had marked a few minutes earlier. Their moment of action arrives as the lead police scout vehicle in the convoy passes the designated cut-off point. With a swift dial of a number, the terrorists triggers the IED device concealed on the bridge, resulting in a deafening explosion.

The force of the blast sends shockwaves through the convoy, causing the car in front of Munir to overturn in a violent tumble.

As the other cars of the convoy screech to a halt, the terrorists seize their opportunity. They abandon their cover to advance towards the beleaguered convoy in their police van.

Munir sees the car ahead in flames and notices a police van approaching towards them. Munir is taken aback. The terrorists hurl grenades at their cars and open fire at will.

The SPG group retaliates to the incoming array of bullets from the police van.

The gravity of the situation dawns upon Munir. He springs into action as he witnesses the unfolding carnage. With a mixture of shock and resolve, he was left with little choice but to enact Plan B—which was to split the convoy in order to evade further danger.

Drago, his instincts honed by years of training, now takes command. With swift precision, he assumes control of the vehicle, executing a rapid reversal as he signals the Prime Minister's car right behind him to follow suit. From now on he would be personally responsible for PM's car..

The convoy retracts, a coordinated retreat in the face of relentless gunfire from the encroaching terrorists. The SPG responds in kind, unleashing a barrage of bullets to hold off the assailants as they manoeuvre away from the ambush site.

The chaotic symphony of gunfire echoes through the streets as the Prime Minister's convoy navigates the perilous terrain. Amidst the fray, confusion grips the terrorists as the convoy splits into three groups and splinters their carefully laid plans.

By default, Iqbal, who is at the steering wheel, follows the convoy with more number of cars. The other terrorist Suleiman meanwhile dials Ovaise on phone and continues to fire randomly at the convoy. Perched atop the TV 365 Building, at Vile Parle (East). Ovaise receives the report from his subordinate, Suleiman. "Cheta, the convoy has split. I repeat, the convoy has split. "Ovaise contemplates the unfolding situation." "How many cars are there?" he inquires, a hint of urgency in his voice.

From the vantage point of the terrorists, a long line of vehicles stretches out along the road, their progress impeded by the ongoing firefight. "At first two cars moved away from the main group, disappearing down a separate route The rest of the 12 cars have also split into two more groups, one of them also has an ambulance following them "Suleiman continues to paint a picture of events, so that Ovaise could guide them.

"It's an old trick," Ovaise remarks coolly, his mind already calculating the next move. "Follow those two cars."

As Ovaise absorbs the scene, a sudden presence startles him. He turns to find Geetika standing nearby, her eyes betraying a depth of understanding that sends a chill down Ovaise's spine. He knows he has been caught off guard, and explanations might not be enough anymore.

Meanwhile, in the heart of the action, Munir maintains a vigilant watch from behind the wheel of his car. Through the rear-view mirror, he witnesses the abrupt halt of the police van in pursuit, a sense of foreboding settling over him.

"Keep moving," Munir commands tersely over the walkie-talkie to the other two convoys, his voice laced with urgency. "Don't stop the car."

Then the police van executes a swift U-turn. Munir's instincts kick into overdrive. Sensing imminent danger, he issues a directive to Drago, his voice crackling with urgency over the radio waves. "They have not taken the bait," Munir informs Drago. "They're coming after you. Protect the PM at all costs. We're on our way to support you." With a swift change, of course, Munir's convoy veers towards Drago's position, a show of solidarity in the face of adversity.

Drago is once again passing by the under construction metro tunnel. The "what if "triggers in his mind. A whole new way to tackle the emergency at hands, crosses his minds, but first he needs to decide, because in this case he is personally responsible for the PM. Inside Drago's car, a palpable tension fills the air, he does not know, how many more hurdles like this police van lay ahead, en route to the airport. Even the NSG, would take another 20 odd minutes to reach from the nearest base at Pune, and provide them with an air cover, but by then it could be game over for them. Staying concealed will leave them less exposed. More importantly, though, Ovaise might not have anticipated an out of the box move such as this, he thought. He decides to trust his instincts. Drago's voice cuts through the silence, commanding authority as he issues instructions to his team.

"Alpha 1, stick with me," Drago orders firmly. "The Prime Minister's safety is our top priority."

With determination etched on his face, Drago's car veers sharply off the main road, and after moving through the approach road for a few meters , he disappears into the darkness of the under construction metro tunnel. The Prime Minister's vehicle follows suit, their path uncertain yet resolute.

As the convoy vanishes into the depths of the tunnel, the police van, recognizing the shift in direction, follows in hot pursuit, disappearing into the shadows cast by the city's complex infrastructure.

Munir's eyes widen in disbelief as he witnesses Drago and PM's car followed by the police van veering off course, its abrupt turn sparking a surge of frustration within him.

"What the hell, Drago? Where are you going?" he demands, his voice taut with urgency.

In response, Drago's voice crackles over the walkie-talkie, his tone resolute despite the interference.

"Sir, I agree these are not conventional tactics, but our enemy is anything but conventional. We must be disruptive. Think outside the box." Drago's voice on the walkie starts breaking.

"Sir, these are underground metro tunnels. Construction is on the verge of completion, but it's a network spanning 32 kilometers......," Drago's voice echoes faintly over the walkie-talkie before disappearing altogether into a static. This leaves Munir and the others in the convoy in a tense silence.

Inside the police van, Suleiman and Iqbal carry out their sinister mission with ruthless efficiency. As they follow Drago's car into the depths of the tunnel, they unleash a barrage of grenades right at the entrance of the tunnel.

Approaching the entrance of the tunnel, Munir and the remaining convoy vehicles prepare to follow Drago's lead. But before they can proceed further , the air resonates with the deafening roar of explosions.

The tunnel entrance is engulfed in chaos as concrete rubble rains down, blocking Munir's path and trapping his car in a prison of twisted metal and shattered concrete. Munir's frustration boils over as he attempts to establish contact with Drago and the Prime Minister's car once again, "Drago come in...Drago come in....Alpha 1 come in .....Alpha 1 come in." but all he gets in return is complete radio silence. They have officially lost contact with Drago and PM's car. Munir grunts in anger.

Chapter 25

Call Sign "DRAGO"

The sound of the bomb explosions at the entrance had reverberated throughout the tunnel, Drago had expected, that the two gunmen would follow him inside the tunnels, but since they did, and blocked the entrance for others, he had to first shield the Prime Minister. The walkie - talkies remained non operational, so with quick thinking, he drove his car parallel to the PM's car, he rolled down his windows, asks the PM's driver designate to do the same and speaks "You will have to take the lead from here. Do not stop the car till you reach the end of the tunnel. "He instructed explicitly. "If, for some reason, you hit a roadblock, stay inside the car, no matter what. Only step out, when I or another member of the SPG comes to retrieve you." The driver gave him a thumbs up. Drago exchanged a look with the Prime Minister, followed by a salutation: "Jai Hind", the Prime Minister responded in the same currency. Drago then allowed the vehicle carrying the Prime Minister to take the lead, and while he watched PM's car continuing to drive ahead, he brought his own car to a sudden halt.

Positioning his car at a particular angle in the opposite direction, he turned off the headlights. The tunnel was still in the last stages of completion, so there were no light installations as such and Drago had thought of playing it to his own advantage. He turned off his own car's service light as well. It was pitch dark outside, and he had done that deliberately. It would allow his eyes pupils to dilate further and adapt to the darkness. This would eventually allow him to see, even in the extremely low light situation like this. His car's engine continued to hum in a rhythmic tone; while he waited in the shadows, anticipating the inevitable confrontation.

Sitting inside this custom made Range Rover of the PM's convoy, his eyes had slowly but surely started adjusting to the no light scenario, but in his head Drago was already pre-empting the potential outcomes. Grim possibilities emerged for each possible simulation. A head-on collision at high speed with the police van carried a staggering 90% chance of mortality. A sideways impact presented a marginally higher 95% chance of mortality, but a lot would depend on the speed at the time of the impact, he thought. Undeterred by the odds, Drago waited in anticipation, while he continued his mental calculations, wondering if a certain angle of impact would be more beneficial. His headlights continued to be turned off, his eyes dead pan, he was committed to the moment, and it looked like he would ram into the terrorists even at the cost of his own life.

A few moments pass in silence, and then the headlights of the incoming police van are finally visible from the far end of the tunnel. It was time to execute his plan, first up, he disabled the ADAS system, so the speed warning would not distract him . Drago sped up with a reckless abandon, hurtling toward the impending danger with his cars head lights still shrouded in darkness. He knew he had to hit the speed of 150 kms/hr or above to make a significant impact. The speedometer was still hovering around the 120 kms/hr mark, so he pushed the accelerator harder and went into a full throttle mode, his cars head lights were still off.

Within the confines of the police van, the two terrorists barreled forward at the maximum speed possible. The van did not have the speed, but it certainly had the strength and tenacity. Suleiman and Iqbal had their senses heightened for any sign of danger. The van's headlights could only see a few meters ahead. They were scouting out for the red taillights of a car in the otherwise dark tunnel. Suddenly, a pair of headlights come alive, casting a darting illumination of light upon the windscreen of the police van. Iqbal, who is at the steering wheel, gets temporarily blinded with this sudden beam of light, piercing through the windscreen .Before he can react, Drago's car careens into the view, skidding sideways at an uproarious speed of 160 kms/hr and rams into the police van with a thunderous crash. The car had slammed into the police van at such an angle that it effectively ended up blocking their path ahead in the tunnel.

In the collision's aftermath, both vehicles lay immobile. The dust was still settling down, but the road ahead of the police van now appeared impassable. Though injured from the impact, Drago finds solace in the protection afforded by the car's airbags,

Using his turtled vehicle as a makeshift shield, Drago pulls out his Glock -17 from his body harness and emerges from the wreckage. He presses on with the disruptive psychological advantage he had gained with the crash. He tries to get closer to the van for a clear shot.

Suleiman and Iqbal were badly injured, yes, but they soon regained their composure. They realized they could not move forward because of the blockade caused by Drago's car. Frustrated, they first shot blindly, and once they recognized Drago's silhouette, in the darkness they focussed their gun power on him. Drago shot back, engaging the terrorists in a ferocious gun battle. The staccato rhythm of gunfire filled the air as the intense gunfight ensued in the cramped tunnel. Iqbal and Suleiman, their weapons trained with deadly precision, unleashed a barrage of bullets in Drago's direction, their intent clear: to eliminate the obstacle standing between them and their nefarious objectives.

With lightning-fast reflexes, Drago returned fire, his movements fluid and calculated as he sought to gain the upper hand, and get closer and closer to them in the chaotic exchange. Bullets ricocheted off the tunnel walls, sending sparks flying, as the combatants continued to engage in a deadly dance of death.

Amidst the chaos, Drago manoeuvred with tactical precision. His training kicked in, his mind sharp and focused as he calculated his moves against the two formidable adversaries. Iqbal and Suleiman, undeterred by Drago's resilience, pressed forward with unrelenting ferocity. Their determination matched only by their ruthlessness. The two parties closed onto each other, with just a few feet separating them now. Drago, ideally, should have backed away a few feet and maintained a strong cover, but fuelled by a potent mix of adrenaline rush and sheer willpower, he refused to back down. Infact, he was baiting himself, to give a sense of hope to his enemies, that the target was well within their reach. And in the next few moments, Iqbal walked into his trap. In an effort to get the upper hand, Iqbal charged towards Drago, even as Suleiman provided him with the cover fire. Drago, in a swift retaliation, dived in the opposite direction and fired at Iqbal. Drago's gun found its mark as the bullets tore through Iqbal's abdomen. Drago pumped two more bullets to silence Iqbal forever.

Suleiman watches Iqbal die. He screams in anguish and his gun power then reaches a feverish pitch. Drago, falls back in the process to draw him in. Suleiman follows suit but then his gun goes silent for a moment. Drago realizes the terrorist was probably reloading the gun. Drago was also well aware that he himself was left with just one bullet. He does not have a clear shot at the moment, and a missed shot would put the odds in Suleiman's favour. He seizes the moment and covers the remaining distance between him and Suleiman with stealth. He knows that victory cannot be achieved through bullets alone. Suleiman opens fire again, but he was unaware that Drago had already moved closer. In a surprise move and roar of a primal order, Drago pounces on him, his fists raised in defiance.

The sound of flesh meeting flesh punctuates the air with a sickening thud. Drago, fuelled by a potent mix of determination and desperation, unleashes a flurry of blows, his movements a seamless blend of offense and defence.

In a decisive manoeuvre, Drago delivers a crushing blow that sends Suleiman sprawling to the ground. Suleiman loses his weapon in the process. In the heat of the moment, Drago springs forward and unleashes a relentless onslaught of punches, each blow landing with precision and force. He continues to rain down blows upon Suleiman. He is relentless in his assault until the light fades from Suleiman's eyes, leaving him dead. This was not the first time he had killed someone with his bare hands, and he would do it again, and again in the service of his motherland if required. There was a reason Dheeraj Singh had earned his call sign, "DRAGO" – he was a pinnacle of fury when provoked. A Dragon, who would spit fire and burn his enemy to dust.

In the dimly lit tunnel, the Prime Minister's car had made its way forward, reaching a point where construction of the tunnel was still in progress, but the end of the passage was also in view. It was literally the light at the end of the tunnel, a few meters ahead. Choosing to walk the remaining distance, the Prime Minister emerged, surrounded by his SPG escorts.

Passing by astonished labourers, the Prime Minister received nods and murmured acknowledgments of disbelief from the workers.

"Isn't he looking just like the Prime Minister?" one labourer remarked. His companion replied sarcastically, "Come on! Think logically. What would the Prime Minister of our country do in a place like this?" The first labourer persisted, "No, I'm telling you, he is our Prime Minister. Want to bet ten bucks?" "Sure let's bet on it " the other labourer agreed.

With a casual salute to the laborers, the Prime Minister continued his journey through the tunnel.

Exiting the tunnel, the sight of a waiting NSG helicopter greeted the Prime Minister, its blades spinning in anticipation. As the Prime Minister approached, a NSG commando saluted and escorted him aboard the aircraft.

RAW Situation Room, BARC, Mumbai

29 September, 2023

1805 hrs

Back in the situation room where the RAW analysts had been working tirelessly for hours, an analyst made a significant discovery and urgently called for Roma. Rushing to the analyst's workstation, Roma observed a map displaying geo-tagged locations across the Middle East and Russia.

"Roma Madam," the analyst began, "based on the information provided by the CIA Middle East Attaché, we've been tracking Ovaise Sheikh's movements, in the last few months," Another slide revealed bank transactions linking Ovaise Sheikh to the Dark Web and Crypto Currency Exchanges.

"We've successfully correlated his movements with some cryptocurrency transactions," the analyst continued. Roma scrutinized the transactions, noting a substantial sum of bitcoins exchanged. "What are these transactions linked to Moscow servers?" Roma inquired, "Madam, that's precisely why we've called you," the analyst replied.

Metro Tunnel, Mahim Bay, Mumbai

29 September, 2023

1805 hrs

Meanwhile, back at the under construction exit of the tunnel, the two labourers looked at the PM's helicopter, getting ready to be airborne. The labourers noticed one more figure emerging from inside the tunnel. It was Drago.

As he walks out, he sees the NSG chopper getting airborne. The two labourers are in awe. They have seen nothing like this before. One of them approaches Drago. "Isn't he our Prime Minister?" the labourer asked, pointing at the helicopter. The helicopter disappears out of sight in just a few moments.

Drago looks at both the labourers and shakes his head with a smile. " No, " he says and continues walking away. "See, I told you he can't be Prime Minister, now pay up, ten bucks!" the other labourer exclaimed. Drago had been eavesdropping on the conversation, so he sums up his incomplete response "This PM is a bit different from the other PM's. He likes to call himself as the Pradhan Sevak, "Drago remarked, as he headed toward the spot from where the helicopter departed. The labourer once again exchanged the Rs 10 note as he realized he had won the bet after all. The labourer's banter continues in the background, and Drago's phone rings.

Roma strode purposefully through the corridors of the makeshift RAW Headquarters, at BARC, her mind racing with the latest intelligence reports. Two seasoned RAW officers and a team of commandos flanked her, their footsteps echoing in the quiet hallway as she spoke to Drago.

"Where were you, Drago? Your phone was unreachable," Roma inquired as they walked. Roma's brow furrowed in confusion. "Never mind. What were you saying?" Drago deflected the question.

Roma updated Drago about the latest information gleaned from CIA and the dark web. "About 2 months ago, in the light of the ongoing conflict between Ukraine and Russia, ISIS acquired a high-value Artificial Intelligence-Driven Weapon System from the Russian Mafia. Code name: Quadath-Ut-Allah." "Fist of God," Drago muttered grimly.

"According to intelligence agencies, the weapon made its way through Ukraine, Uzbekistan, Tajikistan, and into Pakistan." Roma continued, even as Drago continued to make a mind map of the weapon's journey across the borders. "Passing through the PoK–Pakistan occupied Kashmir, it reached Kashmir and was then smuggled out of Kashmir amidst a convoy of apple trucks," she added, pointing to the thousands of apple trucks which leave from the Kashmir valley each year. "We have intelligence up to Nagor in Rajasthan. But after that, we had lost track of the weapon," Roma concluded.

By this time Drago had tracked his way away from the tunnel, onto the main road connecting Mahim Bay and Bandra in the Mumbai suburbs. He, hailed a black and yellow taxi. He quickly got in, his mind buzzing with the gravity of the new intel on hand. "The weapon has reached Ovaise in Mumbai, we can be sure of that," Drago muttered to Roma.

Unbeknownst to him, the taxi driver was eavesdropping on their conversation, so Drago spoke cryptically," *Madari tak pahunchna hai, to saap ko dhonndho. Aur saap tak pahunchna hai to Madari ko. Agar donon tak pahunchna hai? Toh saap ke bill ko dhundho.* "Drago spoke into his phone

Roma, meanwhile, was getting into the car along with her colleagues en route to Goregaon. Roma had by now got a hang of Drago's cryptic way of describing things. She precisely understood what Drago meant. "Sir, we have a lead. We've triangulated the mobile data of the four slain terrorists at the BARC. There's a godown near Film City, in Goregaon East, where their GPS marking intersect. We're raiding it now"

"Great, I'll meet you there," Drago responded. "I've sent you the location," Roma informed him. Drago clicked on the map link and instructed the driver. "Goregaon - Film City."

The taxi driver looked at him with curiosity. "Sir, are you involved in catching snakes and the likes?" "Yes, but right now we're after a rat," Drago replied. "Sir, you're like a godsend fellow. A rat has been troubling us at our home. My wife has been nagging me to get this sorted. Today is the third day, but I have not had the time to find a solution." The driver narrated his version of a sorry tale, underlining the troubles of a common man. "Could you help me with some pesticide or something to get rid of the rat? "the driver added. "If we reach Goregaon East in the next 20 minutes, I'll give you a rat repellant for free," Drago promised. He then moves closer to the driver and places the earphones dangling from driver's shoulders into the driver's ears. "It will help you to stay focussed on the road. " Drago adds with a smile. Motivated by the incentive, the driver pressed on the accelerator, propelling the car forward with renewed speed, but the visarjan processions , were obviously going to cast a delay.

Chapter 26

Catalyst of Chaos

Over the years, The NSG- National Security Guard, has emerged as a stalwart contingency force, poised to intervene in the gravest of terrorist crisis. Tasked as New Delhi's ultimate response unit, its inception dates back to 1986, yet its ascent to prominence materialized following the decisive countermeasures executed during the harrowing 26/11 terrorist attacks in Mumbai.

Stationed in a perpetual state of vigilance, NSG commandos stand, prepared to thwart any terrorist threat or hijack emergency at a moment's notice. Their hallmark lies in the ability to mobilize within a swift thirty-minute timeframe, a unique skill that sets the force apart from other Counter-Terror and Central-Armed Police Forces.

Outside the Mayor's Bungalow, Munir stood surrounded by a group of heavily armed NSG commandos. The lifeless bodies of the gardener and the cook lay nearby, covered by white sheets that engulfed them. Intel shared by Roma's team, based on the mobile data retrieved by the slain terrorists at

BARC, had played a pivotal role in joining these dots, and identify the potential suspects linked with the current crisis at hands.

Munir had a personal grudge against Drago, but he had never allowed it to cloud his judgement about Drago's ability to think out of the box and his proficiency in combat, especially in situations when the odds were against them. The Ganesh-Gauri Visarjan of Ganesh Chaturthi was yet another occasion, when Drago was not only spot on with his analysis, but he had also saved one of the most popular Prime Ministers, the country had seen recently. The Prime Minister was not only a man of the masses, but a leader of global repute, whose cult following on the social media popularity index, far surpassed the biggest pop stars and sports personalities across the world.

Munir's voice broke through the tension, a whisper amidst the turmoil, as he connected with Drago over the phone. "You were absolutely right about the safe house."

Images flashed through his mind of the NSG operatives raiding the bungalow with precision, each movement calculated, each step deliberate. The scene shifted abruptly, and gunfire erupted as terrorists at the Mayor Bungalow unleashed their fury upon the commandos. In a swift exchange of bullets, the terrorists fell, their plans thwarted by the bravery of the NSG.

"With the help of NSG, we have secured the Mayor Bungalow once again. "Munir's voice echoed in his thoughts, a small victory, amidst the chaos that had surrounded them.

"One terrorist had infiltrated as a chef, and the other one had filtered in as a gardener," Munir muttered to himself, a grim acknowledgment of the treachery that had infiltrated their sanctuary.

As Munir pondered over the events that had unfolded, a question lingered in his mind. " I cannot understand one thing. If they had infiltrated the safe house as well, then why did they attack us? "

In response, Drago's voice cut through. "Sir, Ovaise is a devil in disguise. Never ever in my life I have come across someone who gives so much attention to detail. For every move of ours, he has thought of a countermove, and deployed his resources. He has planned the whole thing with precision. He is determined to take the Prime Minister down. "

"Hmm, but it looks like Ovaise's well-laid plans are going to count for nothing, because now even NSG has entered the fray. "Munir recapped the situation for Drago.

"Sir, but Ovaise is still at large. Till the time he is not caught or killed, we cannot be 100% sure." Drago's words lingered, a reminder of the ever-present threat that loomed over them.

With a heavy heart, Munir acknowledged the truth in Drago's words, but also looked at the current equation more pragmatically. "Drago, I think Ovaise has lost the battle, there is little or no scope to improvise. PM, has already reached the airport and he will leave for New Delhi in sometime. "

As the weight of their mission bore down upon them, Drago's thoughtful tone broke the silence. "Hmm, sounds good." He acknowledged, as he passed through the Western Express Highway, in the black and yellow taxi, en route to the godown in Goregaon East.

Drago disconnected the phone and flipped through the photographs previously retrieved from the DVD. He stopped at the blank photo with the Mumbai skyline in the background.

Drago and the team had figured the relevance of all the photos and material, but this photo still baffled him. What could it mean? He wondered.

TV 365 Building, Mumbai

29 September, 2023

1825 hrs

High above the bustling streets of Mumbai, the rooftop of the TV 365 Building, in Vile Parle (East) offered a panoramic view of the city skyline against the backdrop of open skies. Its proximity to the airport added to its charm. It was closer to 1830 hrs. The setting sun cast its golden hues upon the urban landscape as a commercial flight gracefully took off, a routine occurrence in this bustling metropolis.

Ovaise watched over the skyline. He double checked the same with the reference photo he had clicked earlier, while putting the entire plan of **Quadath-Ut-Allah** in place. The view in front of him matched frame to frame. Although he had checked this several times earlier, he wanted to do the last checks before triggering off the weapon of his choice.

Amongst the array of equipment, neatly camouflaged, lay the MANPAD, silently waiting for its moment. MANPAD - The weapon of choice smuggled out through Russia occupied territory in Ukraine, was one of its kind shoulder fired, **M**an-**P**ortable-**A**ir-**D**efence-System. Laced with GPS, trackers and auto propelled by Artificial Intelligence, the weapon system crushed its target with a 99.99% hit rate.

Ovaise stood at the rooftop's edge,watching the Visarjan proceedings. Even his crew pretended to work, while his gaze drifted over the departing airplanes. Nearby, Geetika's lifeless form lay covered by a shroud of black cloth, a stark reminder of the violence that had unfolded. Ovaise had swiftly twisted her neck, and her life had left her body in complete silence. He had promptly informed her team that Geetika had to leave for a personal emergency. Ovaise turned her phone off to avoid any further questions. Film/TV crews often carry the black cloth-Kala Kapda, to manage and manipulate lights on a shoot location. Ovaise's crew, however, had found a new use case for the "Kala Kapda". Geetika's lifeless body was well covered by the black cloth, and dumped in this corner of the rooftop where only Ovaise and his subordinates were allowed. Ovaise noticed Geetika's hand sliding off from one side. It was an anomaly pointed out by Ovaise to his geeky accomplice, Riaz. In a moment of frustration, Riaz reacted to Ovaise's subtle sign, kicking Geetika's hand, to push it beneath the cover, in an attempt to hide the unsettling sight. Ovaise's contemplative gaze lingered on Riaz, his mind absorbed in thoughts, that transcended the present moment." Never flog a dead donkey." Ovaise retorted with a philosophical take.

Riaz, though defiant in his demeanour, failed to grasp the essence of Ovaise's philosophy. "With all due respect, commander, I sometimes don't understand the way you speak and neither can I understand your modus operandi. "

Riaz's actions were driven more by instinct than by understanding. He casually helped himself to a handful of cashew nuts. His defiance echoed his own frustrations. "I don't understand what we are doing sitting up here, while the real action is out there. That way, we would have been just better off , blowing off the BARC. One big blast and we would have achieved our objective of Gazwa-E-Hind- the ultimate conquest of India."

"I can understand your frustrations, brother but unfortunately you are at that stage of your learning curve, where you are going to need more of almonds to sharpen your brain, then to rely on cashews " Ovaise points out, implying the importance of brain work, than leg work in the achievement of their objectives. Riaz feels even more irritated now.

"At BARC, even if we had blown up 3-4 petrol tankers, we would have only had 50% chance to convert it into a nuclear disaster. "Ovaise responded, trying to help Riaz, "Look at the bigger picture." He added. Riaz appeared to be dumbfounded but reacts, nevertheless. "If nothing, we would have had at least 3-4 powerful blasts and loss of many lives. What are we going to achieve by killing the Prime Minister... "Riaz responded with another question. Ovaise cuts him off before he could finish his question. "I choose to stay away from these ifs and buts. Inshallah, I just set my eyes on a formidable target, and then achieve it with planning and precision. "Ovaise roars back at Riaz. "And to answer your question, I think it is more important to make a statement, then carrying out a random attack which would lead to nothing." Ovaise's measured response revealed a depth of foresight, tempered by a steadfast commitment to their cause.

"The current Prime Minister is one of the most iconic Prime Ministers of India. He and the ruling party , are also one of the most influential factors in polarizing the Hindu population of the country. "Ovaise added as he approached the MANPAD. His gaze lingered on another flight taking off in the distance, his thoughts consumed by the impending strike he was about to trigger.

"Today when the Prime Minister will die, then this country's idiots will behave like headless chickens, because for every shortcoming in this country, it is only the Musalmaan they hold responsible. The populace of Hindustan will bicker and fight amongst themselves, and we will add fuel to this fire, in the name of religious sentiments." Ovaise dwells further, revealing the complexities of their mission.

"The next phase of our plan will kick off, after the Prime Minister's death, and in a matter of days we will take India to the brink of an all-out civil war "In Ovaises mind, Quadath-Ut-Allah, represented more than mere violence—it was a catalyst for chaos, a means to an end.

Riaz, finally appeared to be in sync with the complete plan, "So basically, whole of India is our tinder box, the Prime Minister's death, is going to be just a flint, which will set the whole country ablaze, "Riaz tries to rephrase the plan for the sake of his own understanding. "In short, we will bleed India with a thousand cuts." Ovaise simplified the principle of their plan even further. "They are in the midst of Ganesh Chaturthi festivities, but tonight we will celebrate Diwali."

"Alhamdulillah! "Riaz responded. A newfound admiration for Ovaise reflected in his eyes for his planning extraordinaire. Together, they stood poised on the precipice of the building, their actions destined to leave an indelible mark on the fabric of history.

Goregaon East, Mumbai

29 September, 2023

1840 hrs

Drago's black and yellow taxi screeched to a halt. Outside the light equipment godown in Goregaon East, the area appeared to be surrounded by police jeeps and CISF personnel.

" Look sir, I brought you to your destination in just 19 minutes," the taxi driver remarks, looking at the watch. It was 6:40 PM. Drago pays off the taxi driver with a nod of gratitude.

"Sir, you also mentioned about that rat poison" the driver reminded. Drago, nods and questions him back, "*Tamaku khate ho*? Tobbbaco" the driver nodded, and pulled a packet out of his shirt pocket, and offered it to Drago.

"Naa, I don't need it. This is your remedy for the rat. Make small packets of tobacco, wrapped in a cotton cloth and place it in all the corners of your house. The powerful smell of tobacco will repel the rat, and he will not return. It's a guarantee," Drago suggests.

The driver looks amused." Sir, I will definetley try it out, but can you also give me something that you will be using right now for the rat?"

"This is a different kind of rat. It only has a taste for a certain kind of rat poison," Drago responds cryptically.

Just then, a couple of gunshots echo through the air, followed by another retaliatory shot. Without hesitation, Drago pulls out his gun and dashes into the alley leading up to the equipment godown. The Taxi Driver watches Drago disappear swiftly.

The godown hums with activity as Drago strides in. RAW, CISF, and police personnel fill the space, each one armed and vigilant with handguns,and automatic assault rifles. Amidst the controlled chaos, a middle-aged man, wearing a skullcap, lies on the floor, his arm soaked in blood.

A smart watch alarm goes off. Roma stopped the sound. It was time for her iron and folic acid tablets, she pops the pills, even as the injured man in front of her pleads " I know nothing madam, please let me go, I have an old mother to take care of, she is a kidney patient. Please. "

Without hesitation, Drago rushes to the man's side, which is surrounded by scattered bullet shells and a discarded handgun. He visualizes the scene, how the man might have opened fire, only to be swiftly taken down by Roma's single shot.

Roma squeezes the man's injured hand, coaxing information from him. "Tell me where is Ovaise right now," she demands. "I really like it. You don't believe in wasting anytime, you directly go for the jugular. " Drago comments, admiring Roma's efficiency. Roma tightens her grip on the man's hand once more. The man winces in pain even as she responds to Drago. " Someone had enlightened me that time is not a luxury we could enjoy, so I was just following the diktat," Roma remarks.

"That is 100% correct," Drago agrees, and before anyone can realize. Drago takes out his gun and fires at the man between his liver and stomach. The man screams in excruciating pain, but Drago knows exactly what he is doing. "Look brother, now with the fresh bullet wound between your liver and stomach, saving your life is only in your own hands." The pain escalated with every passing second, but Drago had got his attention. "You have got roughly an hour at hand. You can tell us the truth in the next few seconds and you will be quickly rushed to the hospital or you can continue to play, Yes-No, No -Yes with us and you will bleed to death in under an hour. "

Roma and the other officers are stunned at Drago's move. The injured man is bleeding profusely. The man screams in agony as Drago issues the chilling ultimatum, and starts walking away, "The complete plan is only known to Ovaise Sahab, but

I had overheard them talking that it will be some sort of aerial attack. I am guessing they were speaking on the lines of 9/ 11 attack," the man confessed, his voice trembling with fear.

With a sense of finality, Drago released the gun's safety latch and aimed once more at the man to extract the last shreds of information from the trembling man. The guy's body language convinced Drago that he had given them everything he knew. He exchanged a knowing glance with Roma.

"Make arrangements to take him to the hospital," Roma ordered, prompting two constables to assist the injured man. She shifted her gaze towards the other police officers. "Search every inch of this place. "She ordered even as her attention was diverted towards the dog barking in the distance. A dog squad entered the facility in the next few moments, signalling a new phase in the investigation.

Drago placed his gun back in the safety harness and starts inspecting the facility. An investigating officer points him towards the findings. Drago recreates the whole scenario in his head, based on the visual cues left behind.

Drago notices the tyre tracks. He assumes it to be that of a big vehicle like a truck, next to it some red-colored spray paint was lying around. He realizes the fake fire brigade filled with petrol, used for BARC attack, had received a fresh coat of paint right there.

Inside the cavernous space, Drago's sharp eyes catch sight of a makeshift table positioned next to a large dustbin. He stoops down, retrieving half-burnt shreds of paper from the still-smouldering embers. He pictures in his mind eye, a person working on a makeshift desktop, shredding some documents and then burning them so that it would not fall into wrong hands.

As Drago examines the charred remains, he feels the lingering warmth and notices faint hints of smoke. A police constable approaches, offering an account of their intervention. "We found that injured man burning trash during our raid. We stopped him and extinguished the fire," the constable reports.

"Check everything in this dustbin carefully... see if you can piece together the shredded pieces and find something of importance ,"Drago ordered, his tone commanding attention. Without delay, a RAW Associate begins scrutinizing the contents of the dustbin. Meanwhile, the persistent barking of a dog fills the air.

Outside, in the godown's backyard, Roma and the dog squad had made a significant discovery. Without hesitation, she directed the officers to excavate the area.

Back inside, Drago's attention was drawn to half-cut wires and a powdery substance strewn across the floor. He leaned to examine it closely, his instincts sharpened by years of experience. Drago took the powdery substance on his fingertips and smelt it. The scent felt familiar. An experienced set of hands had skilfully put together some IED's -Improvised Explosive Devices. He visualizes in his mind's eye and transitions to the moment that had caused the two-wheeler to explode at BARC, and the explosion of the Byculla Bridge. Drago realizes the terrorists had used these anti-personnel mines and improvised explosive devices (IEDs) in the attack. These materials are not of industrial manufacturing, they have a variety of activating mechanisms, and non-metallic materials, which made them difficult for successful detection even by metal detectors.

"This wasn't just a godown... it was Ovaise's command centre," Drago declared, his voice filled with grim certainty. Further deep towards the backyard, the dog's persistent barking signals urgency, prompting a police constable to rush in with news of Roma's summons.

Drago arrives at the designated spot in the backyard where Roma stands amidst a group of officers. They have unearthed a dead body from a pit. "He appears to be from another country," Roma comments, her tone revealing a blend of curiosity and concern. Another RAW Agent retrieves a crew ID from the body's pockets, revealing the identity of the deceased. "Nicolas Forget, Documentary Film Maker - Crew - TV 365," Roma announces, her words hanging heavy in the air.

Drago notices the logo on the TV 365 Crew ID. Driven by a sudden realization, Drago returns to the dustbin. Roma follows him, even as he turns the dustbin upside down, sifting through the debris in search of cues. Among the scattered remnants, his eyes catch sight of a half-burnt paper bearing the TV 365 logo, a crucial piece of the puzzle. With diligence, Roma, Drago and others comb through the trash, each fragment potentially holding the key to unraveling the mystery.

While looking for the other pieces of the document, Drago's eyes fall on a half burnt DVD film cover. It is Sanjay Leela Bhansali's- Khamoshi.

Hospital, Goregaon East, Mumbai

20 September, 2023

1850 hrs

They had rushed the injured terrorist to a nearby hospital. Freshly bandaged by the doctor, the injured man lay on the table. A police constable stands beside him. "Will he make it?"

the constable asks anxiously. "The bleeding was significant, but the bullet didn't damage any organs. He's lucky," the doctor replies.

"He's not lucky, sir. It's Drago. It's Drago's work." The Police constable responds, "If the bullet would have been half an inch here or there, he would have been dead. Isn't it! "the doctor nods in acknowledgement.

"Do you understand the meaning of Drago? It means Dragon," the constable remarks with admiration. The doctor is puzzled, but he nods. "Inform his family." The Doctor instructs. "The constable responds , that they will have to wait for a clearance from their seniors.

As the doctor exits, the patient's eyes well up with tears. "My mother is a kidney patient. She has to go for dialysis treatment 4 times a week. If the dialysis won't happen on time, it will put her life in danger." The injured man speaks with his hands folded. The police constable looks at him with compassion, but he knows his hands are tied.

"Just inform my brother that I would not be coming home today because of something urgent that has come up. He'll understand and go for dialysis himself... Even a message will do," the injured man pleads.

With empathy, the constable agrees, "Give me the number." he says and then dialling the number, the constable holds the phone to the injured man's ear.

Light Equipment Godown, Goregaon East

29 September, 2023

1855 hrs

Back at the godown, in Goregaon East, Drago and Roma gathered around a mobile workstation in one of the extra large security vans. They observed intently as an analyst streamed through the contents of the "Khamoshi" DVD. They're met with images they haven't seen before–a user manual in Russian with schematic diagrams.

Looking at the Russian manual, Roma made a connection in her mind and reminded Drago about the intelligence that they had gathered earlier from their sources in the Middle East." Intelligence reports indicate that the Russian Mafia, led by a former KGB Operative, may have smuggled that high-caliber weapon. "Roma added.

Drago was focussed as he examined the details of the manual in detail, and flipped through more pages. He realizes that those were the details of a MANPAD- **M**an-**P**ortable-**A**ir **D**efence-System. At about the same time, he recalled the injured terrorist's warning about 9/11-style aerial attack. Drago's brain was now operating in an overdrive.

"Show me the radius of 5 kilometres surrounding the Chatrapati Shivaji International Airport," Drago instructed the analyst. Quickly, the analyst opened an aerial map of Mumbai. "Geo-tag the TV 365 Building," Drago ordered, the building appeared on the map alongside the airport. The building is tagged on the map. And the airport is also marked on the map by now. "What is the flight path of flights taking off from the airport?" Drago queries, his mind racing. As the flight paths start getting loaded, through the IIS- Integrated Intelligence System. Drago asks the operator to pull up the blank photo of open skies from the collated folder of pictures they had recovered from the different DVD's. This was the only picture which had made no sense to Drago.

The blank photo with the blue skies shows up on the screen. The photo looks the same. Roma stares at it and points to the right hand top corner, where they could see a subtle tinge of red. "Zoom in to the reflection of this image. "Drago commands. As the analyst encircles the right hand top corner and cleanses it for a higher resolution, the subtle tinge transforms into the reflection of what looks like the TV 365 logo. A realization dawns upon them. Drago screams in anguish his expression darkens. "Roma, we need all the firepower we have got," Drago exclaims, urgency evident in his voice.

Drago starts moving out. Roma addresses the teams of CISF and RAW. "Only the forensic team remains here. All other forces, move out to the TV 365 Building at Vile Parle East," Roma commands, her tone resolute.

The sun beat down on the bustling streets of Mumbai as a convoy of defence agency vehicles, led by Drago, made its way through the chaos. Their destination: the imposing TV 365 Building that loomed ahead in Vile Parle East and in close vicinity of the Chattrapati Shivaji International Airport. It was the Ganesh-Gauri Visarjan day, and the city was alive with vibrant energy. The bomb blast, which occurred nearly a couple of hours earlier in the old town, was yet to create the domino effect across the city. The police had heightened the security measures across Mumbai and its suburbs, but it could not dampen the spirit of Mumbaikars. Festive revelry filled the air, accompanied by the rhythmic beats of dhol-tashe and the laughter of jubilant crowds.

Inside Drago's car, the atmosphere was tense as he spoke to Munir, who was on his way to the airport to see off the Prime Minister, " Sir, has the PM taken off?" Drago asked, his voice laced with a sense of urgency. "Not yet," Munir replied, his tone grave yet determined. "But he's on his way. It won't be long now."

"We have to stop him at any cost," Drago insisted, his voice firm. "That blank photo of the Mumbai skyline, which we could not make any sense of? It was taken from the rooftop of TV 365 Building. It gives a clear line of sight to the planes taking off from the Chatrapati Shivaji Mumbai International Airport."

Munir's expression darkened as he processed the implications of Drago's words. "Are you suggesting that Ovaise intends to shoot down the PM's plane?" Munir asked, his voice barely above a whisper.

"Yes, sir," Drago confirmed. "Ovaise is at the TV 365 Building as we speak, and 'Quadath-ut-Allah' is the codename for the MANPAD **Man**-**P**ortable-**A**ir **D**efence-System he possesses. "

Munir holds onto his phone in disbelief as Drago continued to speak. "The MANPAD uses AI-driven technology that has undergone rigorous testing in the ongoing Russia-Ukraine conflict. The results have shown deadly precision and a devastating impact. Once triggered, it hits the target 99.99% of times." Munir realizes the nightmare was not over yet. A shrill silence follows.

Chapter 27

View From The Top

Inside the bustling VVIP lounge of the Chattrapati Shivaji Maharaj International Airport in Mumbai, the PM's Chief of Staff and the SPG encircled the Prime Minister in a protective ring. The Chief of Staff updated the PM about the measures and countermeasures undertaken in Mumbai to smoke out the terrorists, while also updating about their plan to safely escort the Prime Minister to New Delhi.

Meanwhile, at the runway of the Chatrapati Shivaji Maharaj International Airport, a team of experts were inspecting PM's Business Boeing Jet- Rajdoot. Originally, the jet was meant to fly out of the Juhu Airport where it had landed that morning, but the terror threat had forced the SPG, to change the plan, and shift to a security protocol under which the PM would now fly from the T 2 Terminal of the Mumbai International Airport. Apart from the usual technical checks, the plane was also scanned to check for any residual electronic signatures, as a part of the security protocol before the aircraft could take flight.

Last of the technicians walked out of the aircraft after the inspection. Amongst them was Sahil Patel, the man who had first reported PM's arrival to Ovaise from the Air Traffic Control Tower at Juhu, that morning.

The electronic display system at the VVIP lounge showed various flights lined up for take-off and touchdown. The board was then auto- refreshed and AI 1 / AIC001 starts blinking at the top of the rack. AI-1 or AIC001 is the chosen call sign of an aircraft with the President or Prime Minister of India on board.

The voice of the Air Traffic Controller came through the walkie talkie of PM's Chief of Staff. "AIR INDIA -1 has been cleared for take- off." PM's Chief of Staff acknowledged the incoming update and walked closer to the PM. He whispered something inaudible into PM's ears and PM responded with a nod.

The PM was about to get going, and board his plane when he hears a bell- A Ghant Naad. His eyes followed the source of the sound to notice the Ganapati Idol, installed near the VVIP Lounge of the T2 Terminal on the occassion of Ganesh Chaturthi. The PM changes his course temporarily, the Chief of Staff whispers, "Sir, we need to board that plane as soon as possible, every minute counts". PM nods with a smile, "This is important too," he responded and continued to head towards the Ganapati Idol, The SPG Commandos ensured that the protective ring around him stayed intact.

The Prime Minister approached the Ganpati Idol, clasping his hands together in reverence. He offered a silent prayer, expressing gratitude to Vighnaharta Ganpati Bappa for safeguarding him. Aware that today's day had been filled with numerous close calls, he acknowledged the protective hand, of Bappa that had guided his trusted men through the challenges. Little did he know at that point that he was still not out of of the woods.

TV 365 Building, Mumbai

29 September, 2023

1900 hrs

Drago's car, followed by a convoy of vehicles, comes to a halt. They are a couple of blocks away from the TV 365 Building. Roma issued swift instructions, even as CISF personnel cordoned off the area. Meanwhile, Drago remained engaged in a phone conversation with Munir, his demeanour tense.

Munir was listening to Drago. He was also in his car now, heading to the T2 Terminal of the International Airport, owing to the emergency of the situation. "It takes roughly 45-50 seconds for a plane to ascend to its optimal cruising altitude, whereon it can safely navigate the skies. But these 50 seconds..." Drago tried to emphasize the threat, but Munir cuts him off. "Drago, I'm well aware of what a 'Kill Zone' is. It's the window when a plane is most vulnerable, and there's no better weapon than a MANPAD, to bring it down. I understand all that, but I am sure you are also aware that the PM flies a Boeing 737 Business liner equipped with AIRCM- Aircraft Infrared Countermeasures and Self-Protection Suites (SPS), capable of distracting a MANPAD -**M**an-**P**ortable-**A**ir **D**efence-System "

Drago spoke to Munir, as he and his team got ready for an assault simultaneously. "Sir, this MANPAD is different, it doesn't follow heat signatures. It's a GPS-guided DOUBLE Barrelled MANPAD. The first barrel is designed to distract the flares released by AIRCM while the second one fires and hits the target. To top it all, once it is fired, a Machine Learning based Artificial Intelligence algorithm controls the navigation of the MANPAD. It is designed to hit its target without fail."

Drago added a fresh set of intelligence. "The field testing of this AI based enhancement has already taken place in the ongoing Ukraine- Russia conflict. It showcased a 99.99% hit rate" "Oh no...", Munir responds, his reaction is visceral as he can already imagine how the PM's plane might potentially come down.

With a sense of urgency, Munir ended the call. Swiftly, he dialled the phone number of the PM's Chief of Staff from his hot dial list. His number, however, is not reachable anymore.

At the Terminal 2 of the International Airport, The Prime Minister moved purposefully towards Gate 11, flanked by his security detail. His Chief of Staff coordinates last-minute flight details for AIR INDIA - 1 over the walkie-talkie, ensuring everything was in order.

Munir's attempts to reach the Chief of Staff on the phone proved futile. Frustration mounted in him with each unsuccessful dial, while he manoeuvred his car in the opposite direction of the Ganpati Visarjan traffic heading towards Juhu. Munir persists nevertheless, dialling the Air Traffic Controller's office this time, in a desperate bid to relay information and take action. As the Air Traffic Controller responds, Munir relays the info in a quick burst, "We must stop AIR-INDIA- 1 from taking off. " Sharing his security detail, with the Air Traffic Controller, Munir explained, him the security threat at hand, "Sir, I don't have the authority to overrule Air India -1." The Air Traffic Controller responded. Munir grunts in anguish. His car, meanwhile, screeches to a halt just outside the departures terminal of the Chattrapati Shivaji Maharaj International Airport. Terminal 2 VVIP entrance.

TV 365 Building, Mumbai

29 September, 2023
1910 hrs

As Drago, Roma, and their forces began the breach of the imposing four storeyed TV 365 Building, their mission took a harrowing turn. Scavenging the ground floor with urgency, Drago's pulse quickened as he realized the terrorists had taken the employees of TV 365 as hostages. More information continued to filter in, as snipers started filtering into the buildings surrounding the TV 365 Building and the communication controller continued to take notes and mark positions of the terrorists on the 3D map of the TV 365 Building, open on his I Pad.

Drago was caught in the cruel grip of circumstances, as he and his team faced an impossible decision to make. The time was running out, he could either disregard the hostages and go for an all-out assault, so that he could stop Ovaise from triggering the MANPAD, or he would have to take a more tactical approach and safeguard the hostages as he moved along. Either save the Prime Minister or prioritize the lives of the TV 365 crew. Drago was at a moral crossroad that demanded sacrifice. His duty demanded him to first safe guard the Prime Minister, but his moral compass was shifting towards the innocent hostages. With a heavy heart, Drago hoped Munir would be able to do something in the given time, and he resolved to rescue the crew first. He knew very well that it was a calculated risk that could jeopardize the larger mission to apprehend Ovaise, and save the Prime Minister, but his morality weighed heavily.

Roma and her forces nodded to follow their leader. The communication controller by now had fed all the collective information on the digital dashboard. And on his I Pad opened the Digital Twin–A realistic visual representation of the TV 365 Building in 3 D. He pointed towards the designated spot near the top floor, where all the hostages were holed up. Drago had already made a counter strike plan by this time. Breaking his team into 3 groups, he instructed his troopers to sanitize each floor from 3 different sides as they edged to the top floor. The first group would lead from the fire exit, the second group would enter from the parking side exit, and the third group would use the backside entrance of the building to sneak inside. Drago, Roma and three more troopers would be the 4th group making a direct approach through the lobby to the top. "*Ganpati Bappa Morya*" he shouted out, and his battalion resonated in unison with the same enthusiasm, "The salutation for the Vighnaharta Ganpati Bappa had now transformed into a battle cry for Operation Morya.

Hardened terrorists Sadiq and Riaz had a chilling resolve. They had ensnared the hostages in a deadly grip. And with their well-orchestrated countermeasures in place, they aimed to sow fear and unleash carnage, sparing none who dared to oppose them. They were now ready to take on their enemy.

Gunfire broke out in the TV 365 Building, causing chaos to engulf the premises. The security forces, led by Drago and Roma, met the onslaught head-on. The terrorists had positioned themselves at strategic points across the floors. Each hallway became a battleground, the staccato rhythm of gunfire punctuated the air. Bullets whizzed past with lethal intent, finding their marks with alarming accuracy on both sides, but Drago's squad gradually gained an upper hand. The deafening roar of explosions reverberated through the building as grenades shattered the calm, leaving destruction in their wake.

Amidst the chaos, Drago's team of 5 fought with unwavering determination, their training and instincts guiding them through the maelstrom of violence. Roma, the steadfast ally at Drago's side, exhibited courage beyond measure. Her marksmanship found its mark with deadly accuracy as they moved from one floor to another.

Sadiq and Riaz were formidable adversaries. In the deadly battle fields of Mosul and other parts of Syria, they had perfected their combat skills. They were losing their men quickly, but with that, their tactics were getting as ruthless as they were cunning. With deadly precision, they used the building's layout to their advantage, making every corner a potential death trap. They were determined to keep Drago and his team away from the rooftop, and their last resort was to use the hostages as a shield. What they had not taken into consideration, though, was that they were not dealing with a police force, but a special forces unit trained for circumstances such as this. At the time when the assault began, a small fragment of Drago's team was already attempting to climb to the top of the glass building from outside.

By now, two soldiers had successfully ascended to the pinnacle, and gave a visual confirmation to their team leader, Drago, that 2-3 terrorists,were in control of the hostages at the rooftop. At this point, Drago, and his team were just two flights of stairs away from the rooftop, and he knew the time for the last assault was near. Drago used the walkie talkie to give detailed instructions to the duo on the parapet extension near the rooftop. They were to unleash a barrage of gunfire from the rooftop, and sweep towards the foyer, and that would be a signal for Drago and the team to initiate a secondary assault from inside.

Shortly after, the two men threw tear gas shells on the rooftop. They quickly climbed from the parapet to the rooftop and fired gunshots. This was followed by a retaliatory fire from the terrorists. This was the signal Drago and his team had waited for,a storm of gunfire erupted now as Drago and his team ascended to the top floor. With the attention of Riaz and Sadiq now divided on two fronts, Drago and his troopers seized the moment amidst the chaos. Drago lead the charge on Riaz, with a non-stop fire of bullets, whereas the TV 365 crew was whisked to safety, albeit with minor injuries, by Roma and the other troopers.

Drago stood over the body of Riaz, riddled with bullets, two of his men reported that they had taken down two more terrorists on the rooftop. Drago rushed to the site, and found the body of Sadiq, and one another terrorist covered in blood. Relief mingled with tension as Drago scanned the rooftop, his eyes searching desperately for Ovaise and the MANPAD. Yet, amidst the smoke and debris, Ovaise remained elusive, and the deadly weapon he wielded was nowhere to be found. Frustrated, he and his men conducted a combing drill on the rooftop for a second time, when Drago came across a big wood framed box.

TV 365 Building, Mumbai

29 September, 2023

1921 hrs

Inspecting the inside of the box, Drago realized it would have been used to house the MANPAD. Moving around the rooftop, Drago arrived at the exact spot from where the Mumbai's skyline was visible, with the TV 365 signage falling on its right-hand side. The frame was a replica of what he had seen earlier in Ovaise's recce photographs. By this time, another realization dawned upon him that Ovaise had escaped with the MANPAD. Drago's jaw tightened with determination; going by the way Ovaise had operated so far, he knew their mission was far from over. Stopping the attack was their mission, but in his head, even if they averted the attack and still could not catch Ovaise, then he would consider the mission as a failure.

A FEW MINUTES EARLIER.

Ovaise was right at the spot where Drago was standing. His MANPAD, was in position as they waited for their time of emancipation. It was at that time, that Ovaise had received a call from an unknown number, he was in two minds, whether to take the call or not, but he knew only his close aides had this phone number, he went with his gut feeling and took the call. "*Haan Bhaaijan*, I am at work today, so you only will have to take Ammi to the hospital for dialysis. "The voice delivered the message over the phone. The code red, for their mission had been sounded, Ovaise understood that their position had been exposed.

Juhu Beach Road

29 September, 2023

1925 hrs

Ovaise had been tensed a few minutes earlier, but he seemed to be in a better space now. He was driving a truck amidst the chaos of the Ganpati Visarjan. In the truck's trailer was the beautiful Ganesha Idol, that was previously parked in the parking space of TV 365 Building. It was replete with all the exhibitive décor of India's Balakot Air Strikes, in the form of two fighter jet miniatures installed in a crisscross pattern around the Ganesha Idol, and besides them stood the unmistakable life size figurine of Group Capt. Abhinandan Varthman, the celebrated hero of the Balakot Strikes.

Drago and his team had seized back the control at the TV 365 Building, and while the hostages were reeling back to normalcy. Drago stood alongside a tech specialist from the RAW team, their faces illuminated by the glow of the laptop screen. Roma, ever vigilant, leaned in beside the operator, gesturing towards something on the display.

"Open up the GEO-SPATIAL INTELLIGENCE module. And scan it for potential launch sites for a MANPAD within a 1-kilometer radius." Roma instructed. With bated breath, Drago, Roma, and the operator awaited the outcome. Two distinct points flashed on the geo-spatial map, catching their attention. The operator swiftly zoomed in on the locations.

"Sir, there are these two locations. They're both within 200 meters of each other, and they both are near the Juhu Beach." The operator remarked. Drago realized he had read Ovaise perfectly. He was indeed a man with a plan, and for every possible move of theirs he had taken his own counter move into account. He was the most formidable adversary he had come across. He appeared like a devil who thought with ten brains. He was the devil reincarnated, he was the Raavan, who would burn everything to dust, if not restrained in time. Drago thought in his mind.

Juhu Beach, Mumbai

29 September, 2023

1930 hrs

Ovaise moved through the visarjan chaos on the road, filtering slowly amidst the moving procession. He kept looking at his watch. He had pinned the exact location where he needed to stop. After moving a few more meters ahead, his watch beeped. He knew he had arrived at the precise spot from where he could launch his final assault. Ovaise then silenced the rumble of his truck's engine, casting a dim glow with his parking lights on, he pulled to the roadside. He disembarked from the truck and shot the truck tyre,with his silencer gun. The tyre went flat in an instant.

Stealthily, he ascended the rear of the truck, blending seamlessly into the shadows. As the procession of Ganpati devotees meandered past his vehicle, Ovaise assumed his place within the Balakot Strikes tableau, nestled inconspicuously beside Abhinandan Varthman's statue. Next to it was the jet fighter miniature. The miniature had a missile prototype with a holder, within which he had concealed the **MAN**PAD-Man-**P**ortable-**A**ir **D**efence-System. "As he took position, he witnessed an airplane taking off and passing right above his truck. Ovaise smiled,looking at the plane, he knew, when the time is right, he will have a clear shot.

Chapter 28

The Kill Zone

TV 365 Building, Mumbai

29 September, 2023

1931 hrs

The sun had disappeared from the horizon by now, the last shades of orange in the sky were also slowly drifting away. Drago is, at the rooftop of TV 365 Building, he looks at this watch and then his mobile. He had received the link to the possible MANPAD launch points. He turns his attention to the view of the Juhu Beach, in the distance from the rooftop. The crowd of people swelled across the expanse of the beach with every passing moment. At least a few thousand devotees were present at the beach, each one awaiting their turn to bid adieu to their Bappa, amidst the waves of the Arabian Sea, while a few big Ganpatis were already in the sea. A batch of CISF men had already been dispatched to check out the two possible launch points of MANPAD, but given the traffic of Ganpati Visarjan, Drago was not sure they would make it in time.

Drago shifted his gaze towards Roma, who was commanding her men over the walkie talkie. Drago cautions her with final words, "Alert our boys on the ground. We might not have enough time." Drago then jumps from the TV 365 Building to an adjacent building one floor lower, the precise root which the two brave soldiers had taken to reach the top of TV 365 Building. Drago does not stop there, he then jumps to the next consecutive building, and then the next, and then the next. Jumping from roof to roof, he moved in the direction of the Juhu Beach.

Juhu Beach, Mumbai

29 September, 2023

1935 hrs

The sunset orange in the sky had completely vanished by now, and the sky had slowly transformed into the various shades of black and grey. Ovaise was in the back of his truck parked on the road leading up to the Juhu Beach, concealed amongst the Balakot Strikes tableau, of the miniature fighter jet. The devotees passing by the truck, had spotted him, they were really excited looking at the tableau, some of them even greeted him with "*Bharat Mata Ki Jai*", Ovaise, had no choice but to respond in same nomenclature. Raising his hands, he said, "*Bharat Mata Ki Jai*" but on the inside, those words hit him like an insulting slap.

Just then, a policeman comes inquiring at Ovaise's truck. Ovaise's truck was holding up some bit of the traffic, amidst an already crowded road filled with the Ganapti revelry. The traffic police struck the side door of the truck with his hand to grab Ovaise's attention. "Move the truck from here," the policeman demanded.

Ovaise was forced to change tactics, he knew this could prove to be a dangerous curve if not navigated properly. He jumped off the truck and with folded hands approached the traffic police. The surrounding noise was deafening, so he simply pointed towards the punctured wheel of the truck, to present his case. "Help is on its way saheb, we will be moving the Ganpati to another truck, "Ovaise explains. The traffic police, looks at him with a poker face. "Get it out of the way in next 10 minutes" the traffic police demanded, and as he started walking further, he reported about the stranded truck on his walkie talkie.

Ovaise knew he really had little time on hands now. Ovaise looked at his watch, and then at the sky, no plane had taken off for the last few minutes. He knew they had been exposed, but he was still counting on the fact that he had done enough, to conceal his mode and instrument of attack. Tension gripped him, nevertheless, and he weighed his options. He climbed back on the rear of the truck once again and saw himself surrounded by thousands of devotees. A back-up plan in the form of a thought tinkered his evil mind. A resurgent smile erupted on his face once again, and a determined look was once again visible in his eyes.

Just then he gets a call from Sahil." *Salam Sahil Miyan, mujhe toh laga tum phone hi nahin karoge?"* Ovaise questions Sahil. "Aree, we had spoken naa, that I would only call when the eagle was ready to leave the nest," Sahil responded non-chalantly. "So everything is set now? "Ovaise questioned to confirm. "Think of it this way, that the next 50 secs are the most crucial moments of your life. You are in the kill zone now" Sahil disconnects the phone. *"Alhamdulillah!"* Ovaise says and springs into action.

Drago, has meanwhile, reached amidst the crowd at Juhu Beach, making his way through the rooftops and small alleys, which led towards the designated area for Visarjan. He keeps looking at the possible launch points on his mobile; he appears to be still a few meters away, and the multitude of Ganpati statues and devotees continue to delay his advance. Never losing his faith in his cause, though, he continues moving ahead. He is surrounded by the deafening sounds of *"Ganpati Bappa Morya, pudchya varshi laukar ya "* but at this point, he needs a sign to lead him further.

Ovaise, meanwhile, is ready at the back of the truck, he has taken his position beside the missile prototype in which the MANPAD, had been concealed. He removes the camouflage cloth from the screen and activates the user interface of the MANPAD. The MANPAD had already been preloaded with a GPS signature. The signal of that signature was meant to originate from inside the plane, and that was precisely the part of Sahil's job. All Ovaise needed to do now is to pull the trigger, when the signal from the PM's plane was in range.

Ovaise becomes alert as he hears the distant sound of a plane taking off. The sky is dark now and he cannot see clearly, but the planes light is already visible in the distance. Drago, around the same time, also notices the plane taking off. He knows the moment of truth is upon them now. Drago continues wading through the crowd, he is at the launch spot but there are so many people, within that radius of 30 meters, that he does not know where to look for Ovaise.

Ovaise meanwhile follows the moving lights on the plane, his eyes are focussed on the user interface of the MANPAD.

It beeps and turns from red to green as the GPS signal comes in its range. Ovaise had dreamt of this moment for months now. He had imagined this in a much more controlled setting, but the moment was finally a reality now, and all he needed to do was seize the moment. Ovaise pulls the trigger and the MANPAD, fires up swiftly, before taking flight.

Drago notices the bright flare left behind by the launch sequence of the MANPAD. The light illuminates the truck. Drago identifies the truck with the Balakot Strikes tableau. His shifting gaze also locates Ovaise Sheikh, who is at the back of the truck. Without a moment's delay, Drago darts towards the parked truck, his movements swift and determined.

Meanwhile, Ovaise tracks the plane's trajectory with satisfaction as his MANPAD locks onto its path. A collective gasp ripples through the crowd as the unexpected spectacle unfolds in the night sky. In the next few seconds. A slight flare hits the moving plane, followed by another larger impact, and the plane erupts into a fiery display. It continues to be airborne for the next few seconds before beginning to plunge.

Ovaise watches the airplane go out of control, with a deafening noise, the MANPAD, launched by him had perfectly aligned itself to the trajectory of the moving plane. The entire crowd and festive revellers are stunned, with these unexpected fireworks in the sky. A collective gasp ripples through the crowd as the plane disintegrates mid-air and starts plummeting into the waters below. Ovaise exults in his accomplishment as the mangled remains of the plane are scattered in the sky, followed by a resounding blast. Taking advantage of this disruptive moment, Ovaise prepares, to slip away unnoticed, but Drago had already locked on to him, and he was closing onto him with determination.

Spotting Drago in his pursuit, Ovaise makes a run for the nearby Juhu Koliwada - The Fisherman's settlement. He knows he has a considerable lead and makes the most of it as he disappears into the labyrinth of alleys, while the festival revellers reel from the unforeseen chaos. A small boat meant for Ganpati Visarjan had been stationed earlier, at a secluded part near the Koliwada seashore. It was a part of Ovaise's escape route, and nothing could have been better than the sea. Ovaise had planned to get away into deep waters under the shadow of Visarjan, and then board one of the pre designated merchant ships, leading to the Middle-East.

Not far behind, Drago rushes into the alleys of the Juhu Koliwada - and watches Ovaise taking the small motor boat out into the sea. Drago was determined to catch him. He finds a motor scooter intended for lifeguards. The motor scooter is tied to an anchor at the creek. Drago shoots the rope, snaps it away from the anchor, and seizes the moment. He onboards the motor scooter and crashing through the waves of the Arabian Sea; he goes right after Ovaise.

Ovaise has a good half an hour ride ahead of him, before he can latch on to the shipping vessel and escape into the international waters. Between then and now, he has to be vigilant of the constantly patrolling coast guards, and even before that, he would have to cross the smaller bays of Mumbai suburbs which would be crowded for the Ganpati Visarjan. In light of such a situation, Ovaise finds Drago in a relentless pursuit, which adds to his woes. As soon as Ovaise notices Drago, he takes out his gun and starts shooting at Drago. Drago ducks the volley of bullets and fires back, but soon realizes that handling the motor scooter and shooting out simultaneously might be a bit of a task in the rough sea. Drago realizes his best shot would be to get as close as possible to Drago's boat and then hopefully go all in for the kill.

Ovaise, meanwhile, keeps firing at will, his attention focused on derailing Drago, then on the water that lay ahead. He had left Juhu behind, but Versova Bay was coming up shortly, and it appeared to be equally packed with the Ganpati Visarjan revelry. Ovaise is distracted, however, and fires another array of bullets at Drago. Drago ducks the bullets with a swift off side movement on the motor scooter. As Ovaise gets ready to fire another round, he is not aware that he has ventured too close towards the side of the Versova Bay area; the boat hits one of the huge half submerged Ganesha idols which are still floating after the visarjan. Most of these larger Ganpati idols continue to be made from the Plaster of Paris, they do not dissolve in water; they do not submerge in the water completely and neither are they completely afloat. You might have heard of the icebergs in the Atlantic Ocean, which often cause damage to the merchant vessels. Yes, the same icebergs which eventually sank the TITANIC. In this case, the half sunk Ganesha idols were proving to be the equivalent of icebergs, for Ovaise. Speak of divine intervention!

Ovaise's boat hits the half sunk Ganpati Bappa Idol, and careens out of control, his gun falls in the water and at the same time it provides Drago, with the opening he needs. Drago, gives one last thrust to his motor scooter, which is drawing ever closer to Ovaise's boat. And then with a decisive leap, he jumps onto Ovaise's vessel, his gun, however, is now lost amidst the chaos. The tumultuous hit with the half submerged Ganpati idol kills the motorboat engine as well. The two men were now at the mercy of the lapping waves and each other.

A brutal fistfight ensues, with Ovaise gaining the upper hand early on. Ovaise goes heavy on Drago, with a rhythmic pounding that does not allow Drago any time to recover from the leap. Then with a penultimate blow, Drago is thrown off balance and falls at the edge of the boat, his body half dangling out of the boat. Ovaise pushes him off the boat. Drago is flailing his hands, holding on to whatever he can, and he latches on to one of the safety ropes on the outer side of the boat. Ovaise moves closer to Drago, when Drago hits him back. Ovaise quickly recovers and retaliates with another blow. Ovaise, also seems exhausted, but he now thrusts his leg over Drago's head, pushing him under the water, while he forcefully tries to let go off Drago's hand from the safety rope, he had held onto. Drago is struggling, as Ovaise attempts to drown him, Drago's vision becomes clouded. He gasps for breath. And there comes a moment when he feels he has almost stopped breathing, the memories of Milind's death, the faces of the people who had fallen at the BARC emerge in front of him. Ovaise, realizes he is very close to get rid of his enemy and pushes even harder.

At this make or break moment, Drago manages to summon a newfound resolve, drawing strength from the painful memories. The face of his dead father, wrapped in the tricolored flag, flashes infront of his eyes. He had promised himself on the day of his father's passing that die he will someday, but it would have to be a glorious death in service of his nation. He had fed this to his sub-conscious mind, over and over for over twenty years now, and he knew that losing his life to Ovaise in this duel was nowhere near the glorious death he deeply desired. He bids new life in his limbs; he lets go off his hand, holding on to the safety rope. He descends further down in the water by a couple of feet, giving a false sense of victory to Ovaise. And then, using the buoyancy of water to his advantage, he thrusts himself out of the water; the force is such that it pushes Ovaise off balance. Drago climbs back on the motorboat, with a newfound resolve, and unleashes a barrage of kicks and punches. Drago knows he is in the kill zone now.

Ovaise by this time had spent himself and was not expecting a fight back, he fights back nevertheless, but Drago manages to double down on his adversary, with some lethal punches on his lungs and then a few more punches breaks his ribs. Drago had killed with his bare hands, more than once, but this wolf, he wanted alive. Drago punches him one more time, with all his might, a creaking sound suggests, that he had probably dislocated Ovaise's jaw.

Ovaise is pinned down, but he is in an adrenaline rush of a different kind. Ovaise laughs like a madman pointing at the downed remains of their Prime Minister's aircraft. "There is no point in beating a dead donkey," Oviase remarks. "My mission is complete now." Drago counters Ovaise with an even more deafening and vicious laughter. "I am finally beginning to have some fun," Drago adds "I am looking forward to your reaction once your bubble bursts. The rubble that you are looking at , neither does it have the PM, nor is it his aircraft. "

Ovaise looks unsure for the first time. He once again looks at the fallen remains of the plane in the distance. They are still burning. "In reality, this is an Unmanned Aerial Vehicle-Reaper. It is almost the size of a business liner airplane and it was simulating the frequency, to match with your Man Portable Air Defence-System," Drago explains.

"If you would have known that your plan to shoot down PM's plane had been exposed, then you would have fired the weapon amidst the thousands gathered at the beach for

Visarjan, and caused harm to innocent lives. We simply did not want to take any chances. "

Ovaise looks confused. Drago, comes closer to Ovaise and bangs his head into Ovaises head with such force that Ovaise's head starts spinning. "Let me help you understand," Drago adds, even as Ovaises head spins in a tizzy. "Do you remember getting a call from your collaborator, Sahil? My boss was holding a gun to his head when he informed you that you are in the kill zone and gave you a green signal." Ovaise remembers the call from Sahil, followed by himself pulling the trigger of the MANPAD and the airliner getting shot down.

"After we caught Sahil, we learnt about the GPS signature chip he had hidden inside, PM's Air India-1. We simply swapped the GPS signature, and affixed it on the Unmanned Aerial Vehicle- Reaper, to simulate the frequency for your MANPAD. " Drago enlightens Ovaise with their modus operandi.

"Yes, the UAV is slightly smaller than the business liner AIR INDA- 1, but it has a very broad wing span, nevertheless. So to hide the shortcomings of the UAV, we waited till it got dark " Drago kicks Ovaise in his groin, "You see, we just adopted your own tips and tricks to get the better of you. "

"As for the Unmanned Air Vehicle- Reaper, and how did it appear out of the blue, Munir sir will tell you the long and short of it when he treats you to his hospitality in the interrogation room. "Drago adds.

The coast guard boat was now visible in the distance. They were fully armed and closing in with each passing second. Ovaise makes one last ditch effort to escape,he puts all his weight behind himself and tries to dive into the water, but he can't move beyond a point. He didn't realize that while Drago was giving him all the descriptions; he had cleverly chained him to the motorboat anchor. Drago kicks him hard under his ribs once again. Ovaise vinces in pain. "I was right about you, you are not one of those, who will tie a bomb to your chest and blow up in the name of God, instead you are one of those cowards who are more interested in sending others, to their afterlife, in search of their 72 hoors."

As the armed guards got on board to apprehend Ovaise, Drago maintained a firm grip on his collar. "According to your laws of ISIS, you could be stoned to death at this very point, but fortunately, you are on Indian soil. You will get a trial, in spite of all the wreck you have left behind." Drago adds. Ovaise is handcuffed by the coastguard and looks visibly battered. He shoots a defiant glare at Drago, as the guards escort him onto the coast guard vessel.

Back at the VVIP lounge of the Chatrapati Shivaji Maharaj International Airport, of Mumbai, which was converted into a situation room of sorts. The PM remains surrounded by the trusted SPG, Munir and other officers on duty. PM's Chief of Staff is constantly coordinating over the walkie. A make shift big screen had been procured in the lounge and put to good use for conducting a closed door conference room meeting.

The Indian Defence Chief, NSA–National Security Advisor are visible on the screen and so are the two pilots flying the UAV- Reaper from a remote location. Prime Minister sits with folded hands in front of them. "Thank you for joining in at such a short notice, and helping us make some critical decisions. If it wasn't for you and our forces on the ground. It would have turned into a catastrophe, and I would surely not have been alive. " The Prime Minister remarked.

The two pilots chime in, "Sir, for the first time in our lives, we are not feeling so bad to see our jet go down." The NSA adds his two bits. "Boys, you should be proud of what you did today. A super expensive jet worth thousands of crores, is not worth more than the number of lives you have helped in saving today. "

Munir's phone starts ringing. It is Roma, "Sir just wanted to update you that Ovaise Sheikh has been, taken into custody by us. And second, the debriefing has been scheduled for 11 PM tonight." "Sure Roma" Munir acknowledges and expresses his gratitude, "Roma, I can't thank you enough for your ability to see things differently. If your team would not have collated the data in time, we would not have been able to identify - Sahil the missing piece of Quadath-Ut-Allah, and turn the tables."

"Thank you, sir, but I was just doing my duty." Roma says, "There is one more thing sir, Drago has not reported back to the base. And as you know, debriefing is at 11 PM "Roma drops a hint of concern to Munir. "Well, you know where to find him, or rather, how to find him? " Munir chuckles and hangs up the phone.

Bombay Veterinary Hospital, Mumbai

29 September, 2023
2200 hrs

Later that evening, Drago, entered the Veterinary Hospital near Byculla. He apologized for being away without informing. The nurse on duty scolds him for being so irresponsible. Drago takes it in his stride with a smile and continues to be busy finishing some paperwork at the hospital counter. Another Lady Doctor, walks out with Drago's dog. The dog is still limping, but he is excited to see Drago. Lady Doctor hands over his dog collar. "We found this strange-looking chip inside the dog collar, "The Doctor emphasized her discovery. "I know,it's a tracking device, actually." Drago just responds non-chalantly and starts exiting the veterinary facility. The Doctor says, "Be careful out there. Rumour has it that one of the terrorists might still be on the loose." Drago nods at her and continues walking away.

RAW Headquarters, Mumbai

29 September, 2023

2250 hrs

An analyst at the RAW Headquarters keeps zooming out from a dot on his dashboard, and as the picture gets clearer and clearer, the Geo- spatially laid out Map of Mumbai, appears on his screen. The operator had been keeping a track of the movement of the dot. The Geographical Information System showed a path of the dot which originated from the Byculla Veterinary Hospital, moving all the way towards suburbs and then vanished after a point.

The analyst calls for Roma. Roma rushes in with a cup of coffee in her hands, "Madam, we tracked the signal from this veterinary hospital, then it passed through the western expressway, and then a few minutes ago it has vanished somewhere around here. "Operator explains with help of the GEO-SPATIAL MAP. Roma zooms into the area where the signal had gone missing. The area is listed as AAREY FOREST, in the heart of Mumbai. "She wonders, what is Drago doing in Aarey Forest? "

Just then, a message pops on her mobile from an unknown number. "Stop tracking me now, go get an appointment with your gynaecologist instead. You will do us all a world of good,by bringing another Gorkha to life. "Roma knows it is Drago. She immediately dials the number, but the number is switched off. Roma has a smile on her face.

Glossary

Chapter 1

RAW- Research and Analysis Wing.

ISIS- Islamic State of Iraq and Syria

26/11 Attacks - Mumbai Terrorist attack of 26 November 2008, carried out 12 coordinated shooting and bombing attacks lasting four days across Mumbai. It remains one of the most gruesome attacks on the Indian soil.

2006 Train blasts- The serial explosions across the financial capital claimed 189 lives and injured 824 people on July 11, 2006.

Pulwama attack- in Kashmir 2019. On February 14, 2019 a terror attack was carried out in Pulwama in Jammu and Kashmir by a suicide bomber resulting in the death of 40 CRPF personnel.

"धर्मो रक्षति रक्षितः"- This is the Motto of RAW which means The law protects when protected.

Chapter 2

Ganesh Chaturthi- The 10 Day annual Festival, celebrated across India in honour of Bhagwan Ganesha.

Visarjan- A ritual of Ganesha Chaturthi, in which the Ganesha Idols are immersed into, a water body.

Bappa- Another name for Bhagwan Ganesha

26/11/ 2008- The infamous date of Mumbai attacks better known as 26/11 attacks

Pan-Beedi Stalls- Stalls selling Pan Masala, Cigarettes and Beedis an indigenous version of the cigarette smoked by the locals.

JNPT Dock- Jawaharlal Nehru Port, also known as **JNPT** and **Nhava Sheva** Port, is the second largest container port in India after Mundra Port.

Paplet- Local Marathi name for the Pomfret fish.

Bhabhiji- The term literally means sister-in-law, but it is also used to refer to even a friend or colleagues wife.

Zomato- A popular food delivery app in India

Tadpatri- A huge roll of thick plastic/Tarpoline sheet

Chapter 3

August Kranti Maidan- August Kranti Maidan is a public park in the heart of Mumbai, which is a favourite amongst the protesters. It is also the place from where Mahatma Gandhi, announced the QUIT INDIA MOVEMENT in 1942.

Chapter 5

Hirsoshima- Nagasaki Explosion- Atomic bombing of Hiroshima-Nagasaki , on 6th August 1945, was the first time, the world saw the destructive effects of a nuclear weapon and it also brought an end to the World War 2.

Fukushima and Chernobyl- They are examples of manmade disasters in use of nuclear energy. Chernobyl disaster occurred in 1986 in Russia , whereas Fukushima Nuclear disaster occurred more recently in 2011 in Japan.

Vighnaharta- Another name of Bhagwan Ganesha where he is revered as destroyer of obstacles.

Chapter 6

Adrakh wali Chai- It is basically Ginger infused tea a local favourite across India.

Chapter 7

Pran Pratishthapana- A small ceremony through which an idol of a deity is consecrated in a temple or at home.

Modak- A delicious sweet made of coconut filling and rice flour covering offered to Ganpati as prasadam.

Visarjan- A ceremony in which the Ganesha idols are immersed into the water, namely sea, river , pond or a lake, marking the closure of Ganesha Chaturthi festivities.

Chapter 8

CISF- Central Industrial Security Force is a paramilitary force which is responsible for security of premiere industrial sites across India , including the airports of India.

Chapter 9

Pokhran- It is the site at which India's nuclear test explosions were conducted in the year 1998, after which India declared itself as a Nuclear Power.

Chapter 12

NETRA -NETRA (NEtworking TRaffic Analysis) is a software network developed by India's Centre for Artificial Intelligence and Robotics (CAIR), at Defence Research and Development Organisation (DRDO) laboratory, and is used by the Intelligence Bureau, India's domestic intelligence agency, and the Research and Analysis Wing

PRISM- NETRA is a PRISM equivalent program of the US. A surveillance program under which the NSA collects user data from companies like Microsoft and Facebook.

Cipher- A cipher is essentially a code, a method of encrypting or encoding information to keep it secret from unauthorized parties.

Vada Pav- Vada Pav , is probably the fuel that keeps this maximum city going. Also known as the Mumbai Burger these days, Vada Pav is essentially a spicy potato patty placed inside a locally made bread and spiced with Garlic and tamarind chutney.

Chura Pav is the shavings left from the frying of Vada pav. Instead of using the Potato patty , the Chura Pav , version uses these crisp shavings of the Vada , as the stuffing.

Chapter 13

Uri Incident and Surgical Strike- On 18 September 2016, four militants had attacked an Indian Army Outpost in Uri. The counter raid by the Indian Army, popularly known as the surgical strike was orchestrated on 28 September, 2016. It was the first of a kind counter measure employed by the Indian Army.

Chapter 14

Souk- A market place. Souk is the word used to describe a market place in Arabian countries.

Russian Roulette-

muzzle against the head or body, and pulls the trigger. If the loaded chamber aligns with the barrel, the weapon will fire, killing or severely injuring the player.

Chapter 15

Kumbh Mela- Kumbh Mela is a major religious gathering in Hinduism, where people gather at Ujjain, Nashik, Prayagraj or Haridwar, once every 12 years to celebrate an auspicious astronomical event. The Kumbh Mela , is supposedly the largest human gathering on the whole earth. 200 Million pilgrims attended the Kumbh Mela, held in 2019. In such a huge set up lots of things happen, and one of the most prominent things that continue to occur is children getting lost and separated from their parents.

Chapter 16

Bhindi- Bhindi is the Indian name for the vegetable, Lady Finger or Okra.

Pujari- A priest in a Hindu Temple.

Maska Bun- Maska Bun is essentially bread and butter served at the roadside stands.

Prasad- A sweet offering offered to the Gods and distributed after prayers.

Modak- A special sweet served as prasad during the Ganesha Chaturthi festivities.

Flora Fountain- A historical landmark in the City of Mumbai, it was built in the year 1864 and features the Roman Goddess Flora.

Jehangir Art Gallery- It is another Historical landmark of Mumbai , which hosts popular art exhibitions.

Chapter 17

SPG- Special Protection Group is dedicated to the protection of the Prime Minister during his moments within the country and outside the country.

Chapter 19

IED- Improvised Explosive Device An improvised explosive device is a bomb constructed and deployed in ways other than in conventional military action***The antipersonnel mines and improvised explosive devices (IEDs) are not of industrial manufacturing, and have a variety of activating mechanisms as well as non-metal materials which make them difficult for successful detection.

Me Yetoy- It is a Marathi term which basically means I am coming.

Lahore Meeting- In December of 2015, PM had made a surprised visit to Lahore to greet Pakistani PM Nawaz Sharif on his birthday. It was viewed as a bold and unprecedented move by the PM.

Ab Ki Baar PM Sarkar- This was the campaign tagline of the ruling party, as they pitched the PM candidate face in the build-up to the 2014 General Elections.

Fir Ek Baar PM Sarkar- This was the campaign tagline of the ruling party, as they once again presented the PM as selected candidate, in the build-up to the 2019 General Elections.

PM Hai to Mumkin Hai- These words were an unofficial tagline of the ruling government in the build up to the 2024 General Elections.

Chapter 20

Sarvajanik Ganeshotsav Mandals- Mandals are voluntarily run communities in India which take upon themselves the execution of a particular task or event. In this case the Sarvajanik Mandals take the responsibility of organizing the Ganesh Festivities for the society at large.

Lal Bagh Cha Raja- It literally means the King of Lal Bagh , and is a name popularly used to denote the Ganpati at Lalbagh.

Chapter 21

Gorkha- The Gurkhas or Gorkhas, with the endonym Gorkhali, are soldiers native to the Indian subcontinent, chiefly residing within Nepal and some parts of North India. The Gorkhas are known for their unprecedented valour, and even today the Indian Army continues to have a Gorkha Regiment, one of the most fearless battalions across the world.

Chapter 22

MANPAD- Man Portable Air Defence System **MANPADS** or MPADS) are portable surface-to-air missiles. They are guided weapons and are a threat to low-flying aircraft.

Nashik Dhol- Nashik Dhol is a new style of rhythmic drum playing which started in the late 1950s and over the years, this style and the players have become a defacto presence across the State of Maharashtra during festive times like Ganapati Chaturthi and Janmashthami.

Rok Sako Toh Rok Lo- It literally means 'Stop me if you can', and these lines became famous in context of another serial blast case in the State of Gujarat, where the terrorists had issued an open threat to the establishment. The use of the term here, is just to make good use of a pop culture memory and use it to underline an incident of similar magnitude.

GEOINT or **GEO Spatial Intelligence module.** GEOINT is the acronym for Geospatial Intelligence, which is information derived from an analysis of images and data associated with a particular location. GEOINT uses imagery to survey and assess human activity and physical geography anywhere on Earth.

CIA Middle East- American Central Investigative Agencies office in the Middle East of Asia.

Chapter 23

Dhol Tasha- A combination of percussion instruments, 'Dhol-Tasha' were primarily used at the beginning of war, to motivate soldiers and the dance performed on it is done with spears. Today, however it has become a cultural expression of rhythmic drum beats performed by a group at the time of festivities.

Takbir - Takbir is the Arabic equivalent of Allāhu Akbar.

Gandhi Topi – Gandhi Topi is a traditional cap, worn by most of Maharashtrians on special occasions.

Marathi Manus- Marathi Manus is a Marathi term to represent the common man from the State of Maharashtra.

Dabbawala- A Dabbawala is *a* worker who delivers hot lunches from homes and restaurants to people at work in India, especially in Mumbai.

Ho Saheb- Ho Saheb is a Marathi equivalent of -Yes Sir.

Naka- A place where more than two roads intersect.

Ajmal Kasab- Ajmal Kasab, was a Pakistani terrorist and a member of the Islamic terrorist organization Lashkar-e-

Taiba through which he took part in the 2008 Mumbai terrorist attacks. He was the only one arrested alive in the attacks.

Chapter 25

NSG- The National Security Guard, commonly known as Black Cats, is a counter-terrorism unit of India under the Ministry of Home Affairs. It was founded on 16 October 1984, following Operation Blue Star, to combat terrorist activities and protect states against internal disturbances.

PoK- Pakistan Occupied Kashmir is the disputed part of Kashmir, currently in possession of Pakistan.

Film City- Film City, also known as Dadasaheb Phalke Chitranagri, spans more than 520 acres in the suburbs of Mumbai and has approximately 42 outdoor shooting locations and 16 studios dedicated to film making.

Chapter 26

Musalmaan- Another word to describe the Muslim population of the country.

Alhamadulillah – It's an Arabic phrase meaning "**praise be to God**", sometimes translated as "thank God"

Chapter 27

AI 1/AIC001- It is the call sign to represent the status of a flight in India, whenever the President, Prime Minister or Vice President of India is travelling on board.

Machine Learning and Artificial Intelligence- Artificial Intelligence (AI) and machine learning are often used interchangeably, but machine learning is a subset of the broader category of AI.

Put in context, artificial intelligence refers to the general ability of computers to emulate human thought and perform tasks in real-world environments, while machine learning refers to the technologies and algorithms that enable systems to identify patterns, make decisions, and improve themselves through experience and data.

https://ai.engineering.columbia.edu/ai-vs-machine-learning/

3D Maps- 3D Maps are three-dimensional visualisation tools, that allows to look at information at hand in new ways. The 3 D Map of the building in this case, refers to the 3 Dimensional structure of the TV 365 Building.

Digital Twin- Digital Twin is a 3-Dimensional replica of an object, replete with actual dimensions of the complete structure.

Balakot Air Strikes- The 2019 Balakot Airstrike was a bombing raid conducted by Indian warplanes on 26 February 2019 in Balakot, Pakistan, against an alleged training camp of the terrorist group Jaish-e-Mohammed.

Group Captain Abhinandan Varthaman- He is an Indian Air Force fighter pilot who had brought down an F 16 war plane of Pakistan Airforce, when locked in a dogfight with his MiG-21. His plane was later shot down and he was held captive in Pakistan for 60 hours.

About the Author

Mandar Bam, a storyteller at heart, makes his debut as an author with *Operation Morya,* a gripping espionage thriller set against the vibrant yet chaotic backdrop of Mumbai. With a background in psychology and a knack for weaving intricate narratives, in fiction and non-fiction space(Films, Tv and Documentaries), Mandar brings a fresh perspective to the thriller genre. His passion for storytelling, combined with his deep connection to the city of Mumbai, breathes life into this fast-paced tale of intrigue and suspense. *Operation Morya* marks the beginning of what promises to be an exciting journey in the world of fiction.

Mandar is also a traveller, wildlife enthusiast and bit of a history nerd, one can connect with him on

Instagram- @mandar.bam

Facebook- @mandar.bam

Website- www.mandarbam.com